THE WORLD OF
INSPECTOR
MORSE

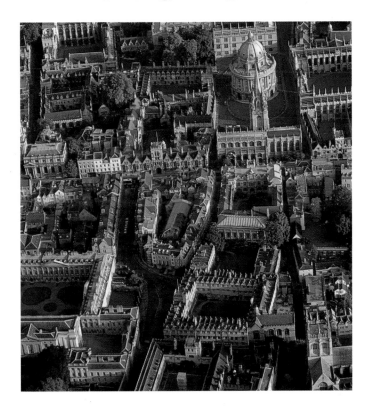

Christopher Bird has been reading crime stories since first discovering Sherlock Holmes, Dr Watson and 'The Five Orange Pips' at the age of ten. Since becoming a full-time writer, he has developed a professional interest in criminal fact and crime fiction, whether on screen or in print.

THE WORLD OF
INSPECTOR
MORSE

A COMPLETE A–Z REFERENCE
FOR THE MORSE ENTHUSIAST

Christopher Bird
with a Foreword by
Colin Dexter

B🕮XTREE
CARLTON

This book is for Flora Roberts
(*sub pallio sordido . . .*)

ACKNOWLEDGEMENT

I owe a debt of thanks to Colin Dexter for his time and hospitality during the preparation of this book. I would also like to express my gratitude to Antony Richards of The Inspector Morse Society, Chris Burt, Sian Facer and Dawn Steele of Carlton Television and Rose Wild of *The Times*.

First published in Great Britain in 1998 by Boxtree

an imprint of Macmillan Publishers Ltd
25 Eccleston Place, London, SW1W 9NF
and Basingstoke

Associated companies throughout the world

ISBN 0 7522 2117 5

Text © Christopher Bird/Carlton Television Ltd/Colin Dexter 1998

The right of Christopher Bird to be identified as Author of this Work has been asserted by him
in accordance with the Copyright, Designs and Patents Act 1988.

1 3 5 7 9 10 8 6 4 2

A CIP catalogue record for this book is available from the British Library.

Printed and bound in Great Britain by Bath Press

Reproduction by Speedscan Ltd

Inside page design by Robert Updegraff

Cover photographs © Carlton Television Ltd by (front cover) Peter Bolton and (back cover) Tony Nutley,
showing John Thaw as Chief Inspector Morse and Kevin Whately as Sergeant Lewis.
The *Inspector Morse* drama series is a Carlton Production for ITV.
Carlton logo copyright © Carlton Television Ltd 1998.

p.49: Lines from 'Burnt Norton' from *Four Quartets*, COLLECTED POEMS 1909-1962 by T. S. Elliot.
Reproduced by kind permission of Faber & Faber Ltd.
p.79: Lines from A.E. Housman poem reproduced by kind permission of the estate of A.E. Housman.
p. 128: Line from Hardy's 'Thoughts of Phena' reproduced by permission of Macmillan Publishers Ltd.
All quotations from Morse novels reproduced by kind permission of Colin Dexter.
All quotations from *Inspector Morse* films reproduced by kind permission of Carlton Television Ltd.
While every effort has been made to trace copyright holders for photographs featured in this book, the publishers will be glad to make proper acknowledgements in future editions of this publication in the event that any regrettable omissions have occurred at the time of going to press.

CONTENTS

Foreword

Luck, in my view, plays a far greater part in life than most people seem prepared to accept. Occasionally the gods smile; often they don't. The works of many worthy writers have, like Thomas Gray's flowers, been born to waste their sweetness on the desert air. I was one of the lucky ones. I was flattered to be asked to write a foreword to *The World of Inspector Morse* since it concerns a character considerably more interesting than his creator. Yet since I have always been happy to take as much credit as possible from anything I have done, here goes.

What I have to say will, I trust, cover both the novels and the television films. I am well aware that the two mediums are, necessarily, so very different; and yet the copyright of 'Morse' is mine, and I have ever sought to keep a watchful eye on the main characters, especially where other writers have been involved. The quality of the films has, in my view, been impressive; and had I to award an Oscar, it would go to the casting-director who chose John Thaw and Kevin Whately to play the roles of Morse and Lewis. Has television affected the way I write? Certainly the decision to make the screen Lewis a young Geordie has posed a few problems for me; but, in turn, the television technique of brief, quick-fire scenes has had a beneficial influence, since my own chapters have grown steadily shorter in recent years! As I look back, I see how propitious was the *zeitgeist* when I was first approached about the TV series. American programmes had been dominating the screen, with their car chases and helicopter heroics. And perhaps it was no great surprise that audiences responded with some relief to the slow-paced, typically English, somewhat cerebral episodes of *Inspector Morse*.

I am a whodunit writer. Most of my colleagues rank 'characterization' above 'plot'. For me, both are subsumed under 'story'. Early on I encountered two of the greatest story-tellers of all time, Homer and Ovid. And having spent many a night myself compulsively engrossed in their work, for me the greatest compliment will ever be the hexameter response from the spouse below to the spouse in bed above: 'Shan't be too long now, my darling – just please let me finish this chapter!'

Unless a writer of detective fiction is a genius of invention (which I am not), there is almost inevitably going to be an element of semi-autobiography, at least for a start, in the depiction of a series character. What makes Morse the amalgam he is? Vulnerability; sensitivity; melancholy; pessimism; ingratitude; meanness; independence; pedantry; cleverness. Morse possesses all of these.

Morse is capable of being disproportionately upset by a good many things, including newsreel coverage of famine (he has now returned his rented TV set), the sight of death resulting from accident or murder, beautiful women and litter.

At school he was more sensitive to the arts than most of his classmates. In particular, Housman and Wagner have remained his greatest heroes (as they have mine). His temperament is melancholy, though far from gloomy. I suspect that as a pupil he was not overmuch amused by Shakespearian comedy but was strangely moved by the tragedies. In the sixth form he first learned (like me) about those 'tears shed for things', and knew that Virgil would be a lifelong companion. Like his beloved Hardy, he is probably more of a pejorist than a true pessimist. Yet he can see little hope for the future of the planet, believing as he does that human beings have a stronger predisposition towards evil than towards good.

Morse is curiously incapable of showing gratitude to his colleagues for work undertaken on his behalf. He expects high standards as a matter of course and is exceedingly sparing with praise. He is happy to allow Sergeant Lewis (on half the salary) to buy nine-tenths of the regular and excessive intake of alcohol which has been such a consolation to him in a lonely life. This meanness with money is inexcusable. But excuses have seldom figured in his life, since for him some degree of independence is paramount. He has no intention of explaining or apologizing to anyone for his lamentable lifestyle. He will never marry. He might just cope with commitment; never with compromise.

He loves and respects the English language, and is tediously pedantic about those grammatical usages not always observed by Sergeant Lewis. The otiose adverbs 'actually' and 'basically' annoy him intensely, but he is very fond of 'whom'. He has almost given up the fight over 'due to' and 'owing to'.

Above all, I wished to portray Morse as a man of alpha-plus acumen. At school, at university, at work, I met people with such clear-thinking brains that I was deeply envious. And it was precisely that extra dimension of ratiocination which I sought to give to Morse: to slide him smoothly into that swifter fifth gear which I never quite managed to find for myself.

And what of Oxford? Clearly, in both the books and films, the physical presence of Oxford has been of great significance, becoming (as it were) an extra 'character' in the dramas. This is not the place to eulogize the city: suffice it to say that it has been a wonderful foster-mother to me during the thirty-two years I have lived there. Whilst I have seldom done any serious research into police procedure, I have invariably done much homework on the topography of Oxford and the relationship between Town and Gown. Morse himself, having failed to obtain a degree (shades of Johnson, Gibbon, Housman, etc!), feels 'in' but not 'of' the University; and this may account for some of the cynical and cruel judgements he makes upon it. But, on the whole, the Morse stories are more concerned with Town than with Gown, and the detailed use of specific areas and streets has been an indispensable asset. In my view, a detective series profits greatly from its setting, and few settings anywhere could be more luminous or numinous than Oxford.

This book is a complete guide to Morse and his world. And into whose hands could such a task be more happily entrusted than those of the present author? I have been privileged to meet him and to talk with him about my work; and it is with every confidence that I leave Christopher Bird to guide you alphabetically, kind reader, through *The World of Inspector Morse*.

Colin Dexter, OXFORD, JULY 1998

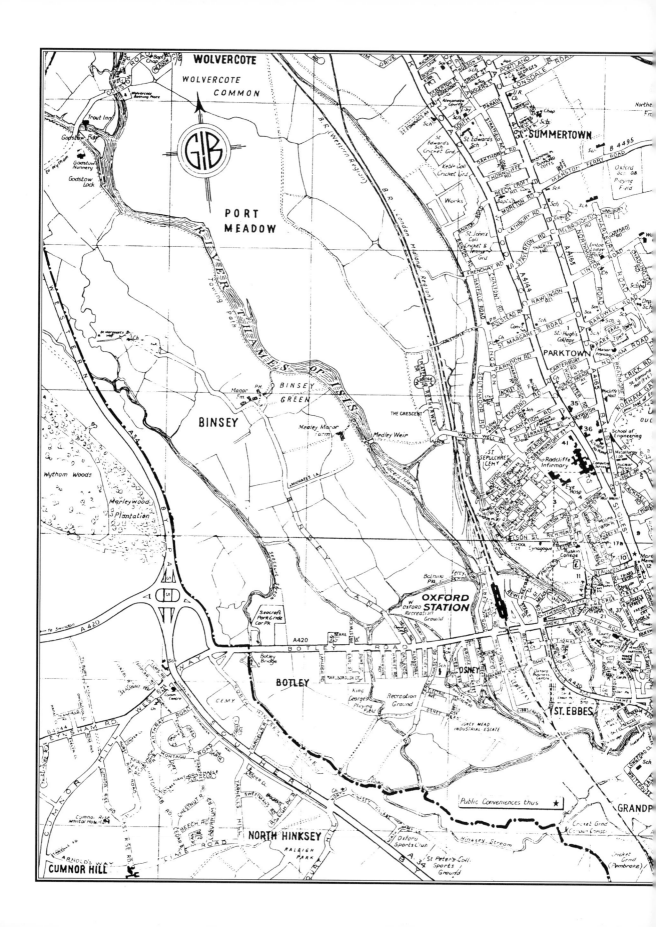

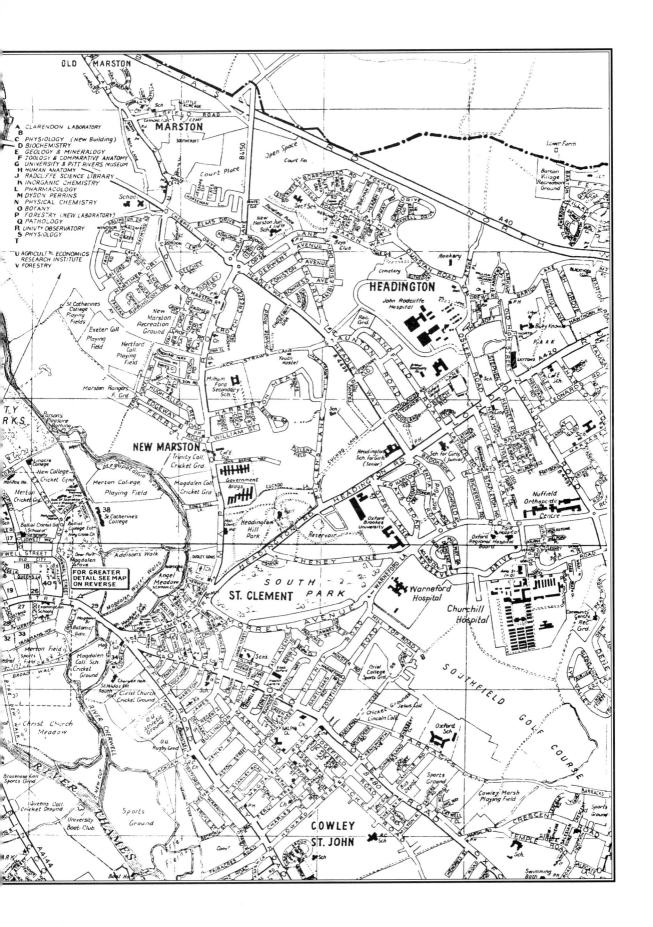

NOTE TO READERS

Cross-references are indicated by the use of small capitals at the first mention in each entry, although the names Dexter, Morse and Lewis have not been treated in this way, because of the frequency of their appearance, even though each of them has his own entry. Likewise, the novels, short stories and films all have individual entries.

When quoting from one of the novels, the chapter number only is given and is either referred to in the text; placed immediately after a title, following a colon; or is given as a single number in brackets after a quote. If no chapter number appears, the relevant quote is from a TV film only. The designation 'TV film' after an entry indicates that the title refers to a film version of the same name.

TITLE LIST

Novels
Last Bus to Woodstock (1975)
Last Seen Wearing (1977)
The Silent World of Nicholas Quinn (1977)
Service of All the Dead (1979)
The Dead of Jericho (1981)
The Riddle of the Third Mile (1983)
The Secret of Annexe 3 (1986)
The Wench is Dead (1989)
The Jewel That Was Ours (1991)
The Way Through the Woods (1992)
The Daughters of Cain (1994)
Death is Now My Neighbour (1996)

Short Stories
Collected in *Morse's Greatest Mystery and Other Stories* (1993):
'Morse's Greatest Mystery' (1987)
'Dead as a Dodo' (1991)
'Neighbourhood Watch' (1992)
'The Carpet-Bagger' (1993)
'The Inside Story' (1993)
'Last Call' (1993)

Additional stories:
'As Good As Gold' (1994)
'The Burglar' (1995)

Television Films
1987:
The Dead of Jericho
The Silent World of Nicholas Quinn
Service of All the Dead

1988:
*The Wolvercote Tongue**
Last Seen Wearing
*The Settling of the Sun**
Last Bus to Woodstock

1989:
*The Ghost in the Machine**
The Last Enemy *
Deceived by Flight *
*The Secret of Bay 5B**

1990:
The Infernal Serpent
The Sins of the Fathers
Driven to Distraction
Masonic Mysteries

1991:
Second Time Around
Fat Chance
Who Killed Harry Field?
Greeks Bearing Gifts
Promised Land

1992:
Dead on Time
Happy Families

The Death of the Self
Absolute Conviction
Cherubim and Seraphim

1993:
Deadly Slumber
The Day of the Devil
Twilight of the Gods

1995:
The Way Through the Woods

1996:
The Daughters of Cain

1997:
Death is Now My Neighbour

1998:
The Wench is Dead

These titles are all available on video from Carlton Home Entertainment Ltd.

BBC Radio Adaptations
Last Bus to Woodstock (1985)
The Wench is Dead (1992)
Last Seen Wearing (1994)
The Silent World of Nicholas Quinn (1997)

* based on a detailed storyline especially commissioned for television from Colin Dexter.

INTRODUCTION

In Colin Dexter's inaugural whodunnit, *Last Bus to Woodstock*, it is Sergeant Lewis whom we meet first. Having answered the call from a pub landlord in whose car park the body of a young woman has just been found, he is already dealing with witnesses in the crowded bar when the duty chief inspector arrives five minutes later. This 'lightly built, dark-haired' man, with whom Lewis has never previously worked, is impressed by Lewis's efficiency and leaves him to gather statements while he goes outside to view the victim alone.

> Morse shone his torch on the upper part of the body. The left-hand side of the blouse was ripped across; the top two buttons were unfastened and the third had been wrenched away, leaving the full breasts almost totally exposed. Morse flashed his torch around and immediately found the missing button – a small, white, mother-of-pearl disc winking up at him from the cobbled ground. How he hated sex murders! He shouted to the constable standing at the entrance to the yard.
>
> 'Yes, sir?'
> 'We need some arc lamps.'
> 'It would help, I suppose, sir.'
> 'Get some.'
> 'Me, sir?'
> 'Yes, you!'
> 'Where shall I get . . . ?'
> 'How the hell do I know,' bellowed
>   Morse.

When Lewis finally finishes taking statements, he goes in search of Morse and is a shade disconcerted to find him seated comfortably in the publican's office, drinking 'what looked very much like whisky' and doing *The Times* crossword.

Right here, in the first chapter of the first book, the essence of Morse is established, long before Dexter envisaged a series of novels, let alone a series of television films. And Morse has brought his creator remarkable acclaim: several Dagger awards from the Crime Writers'

Association and a huge readership. Today there is even an Inspector Morse Society, devoted to studying and celebrating the great man.

The Morse stories are firmly grounded in the classic tradition of British crime fiction where the creation of a 'hero' detective over a number of books is as important as the murder mysteries being solved. Such books have three essential elements. First, there is the intricate plot to be unravelled, testing the ingenuity of our hero. This then leads on to the second element, characterization; for as the storyline develops, different aspects of the detective are revealed and readers can build up a picture of the man or woman concerned. And finally there is geographical location, which, as with characterization, has to be consistent and contribute to moving the story along.

Magdalen College, Oxford.

It is important to remember that Morse's world is an imaginary construct, that his Oxford is not the 'real' Oxford. The worlds of all good novels, however realistic they may seem, are creations. If novelists should fail in this respect, the reader cannot be expected to share their vision. So although Dexter (like Morse) may live in Oxford, he still has to create Morse's Oxford. And Morse's Oxford is, indeed, richly imagined, a fictional territory as rounded and satisfying as Holmes's gaslit London, Maigret's Gauloises-perfumed Paris or the steamy Los Angeles of Philip Marlowe.

Then, in 1987, the television series introduced a new way of experiencing Morse's world. In such cases, the question is always whether books will transfer well to the screen. Here the transition was so successfully managed that overnight Morse achieved a vast new audience. Millions – the ratings never fell below eight figures – were now being invited into the world of Morse, and he enjoyed a hugely enhanced status, entering the pantheon of legendary detectives.

That the TV Morse was not a lesser creation than the literary version is a mark of the great skill and effort that have gone into the films. Although made by a wide range of talent (five producers, thirteen writers, twenty directors and countless leading actors), they have preserved the essence of Morse's world with remarkable consistency over thirty-two episodes, while always expanding and enriching our experience of it. That is why, in this book, I have felt able to assume a degree of continuity between the printed and the filmed Morse. I hope it will be a useful reference work for readers and viewers, and perhaps also for anyone who decides to go and search out the sites of Morseland.

· A ·

ABSOLUTE CONVICTION (TV film only)

This episode brings Morse to Farnleigh experimental PRISON, where the woman governor, Hilary Stevens, takes a liberal, non-punitive view of her inmates: 'We try to think of them as individuals and not label them by past crimes.' Such idealism is treated with predictable scepticism by Morse as he looks into the suspicious death of a prisoner. The dead man had been convicted for his part in a fraudulent investment scheme: money from thousands of small investors was rumoured to have been salted away abroad for later collection. When a second man is attacked in his cell, Morse and Lewis initially think this is a simple case of accomplices falling out over the division of spoils, barely considering the possible role of lifer Charlie Bennett, whom Morse last saw sixteen years previously as a newly promoted sergeant. But Bennett turns out to be the key to the whole mystery. As often happens, Morse's skill with CODES and anagrams leads him eventually to the solution of Farnleigh's mystery.

For many of the Oxford scenes Eton College was used, and the production company was the first ever to be allowed to film in the chapel.

First transmission 8 April 1992
Writer John Brown
Director Antonia Bird
Cast includes Sean Bean, Jim Broadbent, Diana Quick, Richard Wilson

ACTORS

With their good-quality scripts, high production values and two-hour running time, the *Morse* films are a showcase for the best acting, so it is not surprising that well-known actors have queued up to play in the series. The cast is led by the original trio of John THAW, Kevin WHATELY and James Grout as Superintendent STRANGE. There are also three performers who have played PATHOLOGISTS across several episodes: Peter Woodthorpe as Max de BRYN (seven films), Amanda Hillwood as Dr RUSSELL (four) and Clare Holman as Dr ROBSON (three). Norman Jones plays Chief Inspector BELL in *The Daughters of Cain* and *Service of All the Dead*, and in *Greeks Bearing Gifts*, *Who Killed Harry Field?* and *Fat Chance* Maureen Bennet plays Valerie LEWIS, the Sergeant's wife (much earlier the same actress made a fleeting appearance as a neighbour of one of the murder victims in *Service of All the Dead*). Bernard Brown has also acted in two different roles, appearing as the surveyor, Wheatley, in *The Sins of the Fathers* and the murder victim, Dr Felix McClure, in *The Daughters of Cain*.

Kevin Whately, John Thaw and James Grout share a joke during the filming of The Way Through the Woods.

The *Morse* cast lists abound with classical actors. Sir John Gielgud is mesmerizing in his role of Lord Hinksey, the totally insensitive and undiplomatic Chancellor of the University, in *Twilight of the Gods*. At the age of eighty-nine, he completely dominates every scene he plays and thoroughly enjoys himself. He heads a list of the finest British actors who have played supporting roles in *Morse* films, including Jean Anderson (*Twilight of the Gods*), Alun Armstrong (*Happy Families*), John Bird (*The Sins of the Fathers*), Avis Bunnage (*The Settling of the Sun*), Simon Callow (*The Wolvercote Tongue*), Kenneth Colley (*Second Time Around*), Kenneth Cranham (*The Wolvercote Tongue*), Iain Cuthbertson (*Masonic Mysteries*), Isabel Dean (*The Sins of the Fathers*), Maurice Denham (*Fat Chance*), Fabia Drake (*Last Bus to Woodstock*), Adrian Dunbar (*Dead on Time*), Sheila Gish (*Twilight of the Gods*), Richard Griffiths (*The Day of the Devil*), Michael Hordern (*Service of All the Dead*), Freddie Jones (*Who Killed Harry Field?*), Martin Jarvis (*Greeks Bearing Gifts*), Geraldine James (*Who Killed Harry Field?*), Lionel Jeffries (*The Sins of the Fathers*), Barbara Leigh-Hunt (*The Infernal Serpent*), James Laurenson (*The Dead of Jericho*), Patrick Malahide (*Driven to Distraction*), Anna Massey (*Happy Families*), Daniel Massey (*Deceived by Flight*), Richard Pasco (*Dead on Time*), Robert Stephens (*The Settling of the Sun*), Janet Suzman (*Deadly Slumber*) and Benjamin Whitrow (*The Daughters of Cain*).

The role of playing with Morse's susceptible heart has been a rewarding experience for actresses. Many beautiful women have taken his fancy over the years, including Eve Adam (*Greeks Bearing Gifts*), Frances Barber (*The Death of the Self*), Anna Calder-Marshall (*The Settling of the Sun*), Cheryl Campbell (*The Infernal Serpent*), Joanna David (*Dead on Time*), Diane Fletcher (*Masonic Mysteries*), Barbara Flynn (*The Silent World of Nicholas Quinn*), Gemma Jones (*The Dead of Jericho*), Judy Loe (*Death is Now My Neighbour*), Phyllis Logan (*The Daughters of Cain*), Angela Morant (*Service of All the Dead*), Madeleine Newton (*Masonic Mysteries*), Diana Quick (*Absolute Conviction*), Mary Jo Randle (*Driven to Distraction*), Frances Tomelty (*Last Seen Wearing*), Harriet Walter (*The Day of the Devil*) and Zoë Wanamaker (*Fat Chance*).

Barbara Flynn as Morse's inamorata in The Silent World of Nicholas Quinn.

The villainous roles have also provided fine opportunities for actors to stretch themselves. Some of the best have been Keith Allen (*The Day of the Devil*), Richard Briers (*Death is Now My Neighbour*), Jim Broadbent (*Absolute Conviction*), Brian Cox (*Deadly Slumber*), Barry Foster (*The Last Enemy*), Robert Hardy (*Twilight of the Gods*), Patricia Hodge (*The Ghost in the Machine*), Ian McDiarmid (*Masonic Mysteries*), Peter McEnery (*Last Seen Wearing*), Mel Martin (*The Secret of Bay 5B*), Geoffrey Palmer (*The Infernal Serpent*), Norman Rodway (*Deceived by Flight*), David Ryall (*Driven to Distraction*), Patrick Troughton (*The Dead of Jericho*), Vania Vilers (*Who Killed Harry Field?*) and Andrew Wilde (*The Secret of Bay 5B*).

Richard Briers as Sir Clixby Bream in Death is Now My Neighbour.

Morse films are good places in which to spot the early appearances of actors who have subsequently become famous in other roles. Richard Wilson, the curmudgeonly Victor Meldrew in *One Foot in the Grave*, appears as a convict in *Absolute Conviction*. Martin Clunes, one of the *Men Behaving Badly*, is murdered in *Happy Families*, which also featured Charlotte Coleman, who was later to make a big impact in the successful British film *Four Weddings and a Funeral*. Another British film to rock Hollywood, *The Full Monty*, starred Tom Wilkinson, who made a *Morse* appearance in *The Infernal Serpent*, while a young Elizabeth Hurley appears as a schoolgirl in *Last Seen Wearing*. Others who have made a big success in television roles since appearing in *Morse* include Amanda Burton (*The Settling of the Sun*) of *Silent Witness*, Sean Bean (*Absolute Conviction*) of *Sharpe* and Christopher Ecclestone (*Second Time Around*), who starred in *Our Friends in the North*. When Sharon Maughan appeared in *Morse*, she was already a household face for her Gold Blend coffee advertisements, and one of her lines in *Deceived By Flight* was, 'This is coffee – I hate coffee. It gives me a headache.' Soap stars who have been cast in *Morse* include Roberta Taylor (*The Wolvercote Tongue*) and Gavin Richards (*The Day of the Devil*), who play the hard-drinking couple, Irene and Terry, in *EastEnders*, and Philip Middlemiss (*The Settling of the Sun*), who plays Des Barnes in *Coronation Street*. Sorcha Cusack, Morse's half-sister Joyce in the tragic *Cherubim and Seraphim*, later became established as the compassionate Sister Kate in the BBC's *Casualty*.

AFRICA, WEST

Morse spends two months there in the late 1970s on police secondment, and so misses the first dramatic murder and suicide at ST FRIDESWIDE'S CHURCH in central Oxford, which he belatedly clears up in *Service of All the Dead*. What Morse was doing in Africa is unrecorded and remains the subject of fascinating speculation, but it is hard to believe that he remained good-humoured for very long in one of the world's most inhospitable climates, whether measured meteorologically or politically.

ALCOHOL

Beer is not just beer to Morse, it is 'pure FOOD', the source of most of his intake of calories. He has always liked beer. In *The Settling of the Sun* we hear that, as an undergraduate in the 1950s, he was a member of a university society known as SPARTA (the Society for the Promotion of Real Traditional Ale), a precursor of CAMRA (the Campaign for Real Ale), which was to become a very successful movement twenty years later and whose early members included Colin Dexter. As a young man then (and on probably the only occasion in his life), Morse had opinions that were considerably ahead of their time.

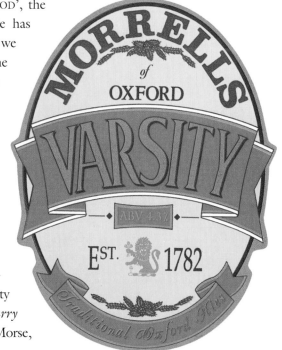

Otherwise he favours whisky, with a particular liking for a single malt. 'Malt too peaty for you?' asks Ian Matthews in *Who Killed Harry Field*? 'I'm getting used to it,' replies Morse,

Beer is essential to Morse's thought-processes. But is he an alcoholic?

contentedly draining his glass. He knows his malt whisky brands – when he spots a bottle of the almost invisibly obscure Glen Duich in *The Secret of Bay 5B*, he observes, 'Most of this goes for export nowadays' – but his favourite is the more easily available Glenfiddich. However, whether it's beer or whisky, Morse is not a fanatic or an activist about brands and labels. With whisky he is happy enough to take a humble glass of Bell's and with beer his preference for real ale is hardly shouted from the rooftops: 'Without being doctrinaire about what he was prepared to drink, Morse preferred a flat pint to the fizzy keg that most breweries, misguidedly in his view, were now producing' (*Last Seen Wearing*: 3). Indeed, for him the real pleasure in drinking concerns not so much the quality (agreeable though this is) as the effect of the alcohol consumed. As an EPIGRAPH to *Death is Now My Neighbour*, Dexter uses an apposite line from Aristophanes which sums up the value alcohol has for Morse: 'Quickly, bring me a beaker of wine, so that I may wet my mind and say something clever.'

By the same token, the inability to get drunk would for him be a worrying indication that the spirit is shrivelling. In *The Jewel That Was Ours*: 24 the Chief Inspector quotes a line of Kipling from one of Morse's favourite short stories: 'When the liquor does not take hold the soul of a man is rotten in him.' Although Morse does not believe in the idea of the soul as it is presented in formal RELIGION, he would understand the role which alcohol plays in many religious rituals.

The real beer-bore drinks the stuff for its own sake. Not Morse. He imbibes because it takes him to places which other real-ale drinkers fail to reach. For, in a skinful of bitter, Morse finds something which would surprise and might dismay many a member of a rugby club: 'His imagination was almost invariably fired by beer, especially beer in considerable quantities' (*The Silent World of Nicholas Quinn*: 6). It is therefore a vital intellectual stimulus for his work. In almost every Morse novel at a certain point, when he is either floundering in despair at the complexities of the case or poised on the edge of solving it, he will send Lewis away to re-interview a witness or re-read the files while he, repairing to the pub, will sit alone with a pint and think. For Sherlock Holmes, it took three pipes; Morse's are usually three-pint problems.

Is Morse an alcoholic? He undoubtedly shows many of the danger signs. He thinks a lot about his drink, drinks faster than others, finds it hard to refuse a drink when one is offered, is convinced he performs better socially and at work when drinking and finds that others, especially his boss, Superintendent STRANGE, disapprove of his drinking. On the other hand, the real alcoholic's most fundamental problem is that drink steadily and mercilessly saps the fabric of their life. Although Morse suffers three debilitating HEALTH crises, each of them drink-related, it would be harder to show that beer and whisky are really destroying his chances of happiness. 'The secret of a happy life,' he tells Lewis in *The Silent World of Nicholas Quinn*: 6, 'is to know when to stop and then go that little bit further.' And in *The Secret of Annexe 3*: 33 he has the following exchange with Lewis, denying his alcoholism. ' "I'm a dipsomaniac." "What's the difference?" Morse pondered for a while. "I think an alcoholic is always trying to *give up* drink." '

The question of Morse's possible alcoholism must therefore remain open.

See also MORSE'S LAW.

ARCHERS, THE

One of Morse's addictions is to this long-running radio soap opera – 'the everyday story of country folk', as it used to be described – whose origins are buried in the late 1940s and whose heyday was the mid-1950s. Lewis is under standing instructions that he can call Morse at home at any time except when the programme is being broadcast.

ARISTOTLE

For the next five minutes he stared vacantly through the window in the pose of Rodin's *Aristotle*; and at the end of that time he lifted his eyebrows slightly and nodded slowly to himself: it was time to get moving. (*Last Seen Wearing*: 24)

Although Dexter clearly has Rodin's *The Thinker* in mind here, the fact that he sees the famous statue as Aristotle tells us much about his conception of Morse. The ancient Greek philosopher Aristotle (384–322 BC) is one of Morse's great HEROES. Morse will frequently say, 'We must apply Aristotelian logic, Lewis', and even more often will measure the state of things against the ideal of the 'Aristotelian balance', which he learned about at school and as an undergraduate at Oxford.

This regard for balance is essential to Morse's understanding of what is good and right. Like Aristotle, he is far from being a pure intellectual, giving equal weight to the demands of the senses and of the intellect – the body and the mind. Aristotle placed great emphasis in his

Aristotle *as visualized by Rembrandt in 1653.*

thought on observation; it was more important in his view than exact measurement, which left too little room for imagination. This chimes exactly with Morse's temperament and his technique as a detective. He is often at odds with the scientists around him because of their refusal to recognize the value of informed intuition.

In politics, too, Morse goes along with Aristotle. His fear of disorder and the mob, his dislike of aristocracy and the power of wealth, and his preference for a middle-class, moderate type of government are strongly Aristotelian.

There is perhaps one additional reason – an unconscious one? – for Aristotle's hold over Morse: in cockney rhyming slang, 'Aristotle' is the word for bottle.

ARNOLD COLLEGE

This is the fictional college whose old boys form the Clarets CRICKET team in *Deceived by Flight*, and it is in a college guest room that one member of the team, Morse's friend Anthony Donn, is murdered.

ART

Morse has a wide knowledge of MUSIC and LITERATURE but is apparently less at home in the world of art and antiques. He owns, on his own account (in 'Neighbourhood Watch'), only one fine antique, a nest of Chippendale tables. In several of the films we see at his flat a brass armillary sphere. This astronomical instrument, beautifully made though primitive in its application, is sixteenth century in origin, but Morse's must be a reproduction or it would be extremely valuable.

In *Who Killed Harry Field?*, Morse and Lewis investigate the death of a painter. Field's work puzzles Morse, though he knows enough to regard it as unreliable evidence, telling Lewis, 'Painters have an annoying habit of painting what they see rather than what is actually there, I'm afraid.' He is forced to seek expert assistance from his friend Ian Matthews to evaluate Field's work. Matthews tells him that the painting is no good – derivative and poorly painted. On the other hand, Harry's father, Harry senior, is a painter with real skill. Without this opinion, Morse would not have cracked the case.

On the other hand, Morse does have some surprisingly detailed knowledge of Victorian art, the Pre-Raphaelites in particular. In *The Secret of Bay 5B*, the Pre-Raphaelite collector Pierce tries to give him a small lecture and is cut short:

The Woodman's Daughter *by Sir John Everett Millais (1829–96), painted in 1851.*

PIERCE: It's, er, it's unusual for him. It's early. You see, Inchbold generally went in for . . .
MORSE: (*curtly*) Yes, I'm aware of what Inchbold generally went in for, sir!

The 'Inchbold' in question is, of course, a fake and Morse knows it. As he later tells Lewis, 'If that's an Inchbold, even an early Inchbold, then I'm the next Chief Constable.'

In *The Way Through the Woods* the 'Swedish maiden verses', which Morse himself has written, draws imagery from a painting, *The Woodcutter's Daughter*, by Sir John Everett Millais. In the film, the verses are discarded by the scriptwriter. But the picture clue is retained in the form of a postcard which the 'murdered' woman, whose body Morse thinks is in WYTHAM WOODS, was carrying in her pack. It contains the message 'I look forward to seeing you here again.' Morse explains his thinking to Lewis:

MORSE: Unlike some, Millais was minutely accurate in his research. I had a feeling there was some specific Oxford connection, so I got hold of a book on the Pre-Raphaelites.

LEWIS: What's that got to do with 'here'?

MORSE: I quote: 'Mrs Joanna Matthews, a friend of the artist, wrote in her diary of 1850 that Millais was hard at work painting the background of his picture from nature *in Wytham Woods.*'

The more commercial type of Victorian art is also familiar to Morse and he easily spots an example of the work of Sir Lawrence Alma-Tadema on the walls of HANBURY HALL in *The Ghost in the Machine.*

The source of Morse's interest in the Pre-Raphaelites and Alma-Tadema's smooth, softly pornographic 'slave girl' art is not recorded.

An Apodyterium *by Sir Lawrence Alma-Tadema (1836–1912).*

'AS GOOD AS GOLD' (short story, 1994)

In this story (originally commissioned for a commercial promotion by Kodak Ltd), a vital item of surveillance evidence has been gathered as part of the case against Muldoon, a terrorist in custody: a photograph showing him entering a flat where bombs were later found. Or rather, the police *had* the photograph. Detective Constable Watson has lost it and Morse and Lewis have been asked by DI Crawford to help with a ruse that will return Muldoon unwittingly to the flat all for, as it were, a reshoot of the incriminating pictures. Suppressing his scruples, Morse agrees to help, though he knows the price he will pay if STRANGE gets wind of this clear example of the manufacture of evidence. The plan, designed to exploit the accused's known penchant for PORNOGRAPHY (not the least of its attractions for Morse himself), is a near-disaster but Morse has a friend – 'a wizard with a camera' – who is able to supply fakery so flawless that the scheme can be pulled out of the fire. In the event, the whole exercise is rendered academic when Muldoon turns Queen's evidence, but Morse is left pondering whether the evidence, if used, would have been a betrayal of public trust. Was this a perversion of justice? Or was it a perverse kind of justice, and so better than no justice at all?

ASHMOLEAN MUSEUM, THE

On the corner of St Giles' and Beaumont Street, the Ashmolean is the setting for several scenes in *The Wolvercote Tongue*, for the Tongue is a component of an ornamental Anglo-Saxon belt buckle, whose other element is in the museum. The Ashmolean, which pre-dates the British Museum by sixty years, is the oldest museum in Britain. It is also one of the major museums of the world. An even more notorious crime was committed here in 1776, when Jean-Paul Marat, later the French revolutionary leader, who himself ended up the victim of a celebrated murder, stole part of a gold chain and received a sentence of five years in the hulks.

AUSTRALIA

See PROMISED LAND.

Morse and Dr Kemp visit the Ashmolean in The Wolvercote Tongue.

· B ·

BEAR INN

This historic Oxford PUBLIC HOUSE, dating back to 1242, stands at the junction of Alfred Street and Blue Boar Street. Morse goes there in *Death is Now My Neighbour*: 14 to consult real-life landlords Steven and Sonya Lowbridge in the hope of getting some information on a man in a photograph who is wearing a particular tie. As the Bear has a famous collection of ties from every type of regiment, institution, club and organization all over the world, Morse thinks he might be able to identify the tie in the snapshot, while enjoying a pint or two of Burton Ale.

It is a forlorn hope. He enjoys his drink, but as there are more than 5,000 ties on display, this makes the exercise 'a bit like a farmer looking for a lost contact lens in a ploughed field'. Then Sonya Lowbridge returns from a shopping expedition.

'That what you're looking for?'

She pointed to the tie in the photograph.

Morse nodded. 'That's it.'

'But I can tell you where you can find that.'

'You can?' Morse's eyes were suddenly wide, his mouth suddenly dry.

'Yep! I was looking for a tie for Steve's birthday. And you'll find one just like that in the tie-rack in Marks and Spencer's.'

BEAUFORT COLLEGE

The setting for the fine film *The Infernal Serpent*, which was shot almost entirely in Oxford, is partly University College and partly Merton. Morse comments on it, 'It's always been very rich, Beaufort. Very rich, very scientific, very musical.'

BEAUMONT COLLEGE

This fictional college is the setting for *The Last Enemy*. Morse attends lunch here – he had known the Master, Sir Alexander Reece (Barry Foster), at university many years earlier. Morse is deadly bored by the conversation at High Table which consists, as he later reports to Lewis, of a distinguished chemist on one side telling him about his piles and a world-famous mathematician on the other who can talk only about his wife's problems finding suitable *au pair* girls.

Beaumont – in reality Brasenose College.

BEER

See ALCOHOL *and* SINS OF THE FATHERS, THE.

BELL, CHIEF INSPECTOR, OF OXFORD CITY POLICE

In two of the early novels, Inspector Bell appears as Morse's foil – a conventional by-the-book copper who contrasts vividly with Morse's brilliant but unorthodox style. Our first brief meeting with him is in *Last Bus to Woodstock*: 24, when he attends the suicide of Margaret Crowther. Bell belongs to the Oxford City Police, based at St Aldate's in the centre of the city – not to be confused with the Thames Valley force, based at KIDLINGTON, to whose CID Morse belongs.

Bell's first substantial appearance is in *Service of All the Dead* – Dexter's novel rather than the film. The original crime at ST FRIDESWIDE'S had been committed while Morse was out in West AFRICA and Bell, now promoted to Chief Inspector, was the officer in charge of the case. Bell's hostility when Morse asks for details of the investigation seems a form of amiable banter, for Bell accommodates Morse readily enough in the end.

Bell's role in *The Dead of Jericho* is even more significant. Again he is appointed to investigate a case, this time two deaths in JERICHO in which Morse is interested. Bell has respect for Morse: in *The Dead of Jericho*: 3 he calls him 'the cleverest bugger I've ever met. I'm not saying he's always right, though – God, no! But he usually seems to be able to see things, I don't know, half a dozen moves ahead of the rest of us.' Bell compensates for his own relative short-sightedness with thoroughness and professionalism.

In the TV film Bell is nicely played by Norman Jones. Anthony Minghella's adaptation sharpens the edge to Bell's characterization – so coffee-addicted he is never without his own Thermos flasks and weary of the squalor a policeman has to deal with every day. Being the first *Morse* film, it is through Bell's eyes that we first see Morse's abilities as a policeman:

BELL : Morse, you know who he is, don't you?

LEWIS: Aye, I know of him, yes, sir.

BELL: Wandering around Jericho, eh? I often wondered what he did all night. Besides the booze.

LEWIS: I've heard he's meant to be a very clever man.

BELL: Is he? *I've* heard he's after the Superintendent's job. And I don't like that, Lewis. Do you know why?

LEWIS: Yes, sir.

BELL: Yes, sir. Because someone else we know is after it and all. Someone who's pigsick of evenings like this.

In fact, Morse is ambivalent about the promotion but desperate to investigate Anne Staveley's death. When Bell gets the promotion and Morse is put in charge of the Jericho killings, both men are happy.

BLACKWELL'S BOOKSHOP

With its main premises on Broad Street, this is one of the largest bookshops in Europe and an Oxford institution. Scenes in *The Dead of Jericho* and *Who Killed Harry Field?* were filmed here.

BODLEIAN LIBRARY, THE

As Jan Morris says in her book on the city, Oxford is built on books and the foundation stone is the Bodleian. It stands both literally and metaphorically at the centre of academic Oxford, with an imposing entrance on the west side of the Quadrangle of the Schools. Dating back to the sixteenth century, the Bodleian is one of the three English copyright libraries (the others being the British Library in London and the Cambridge University

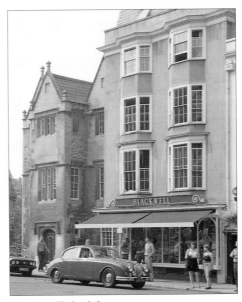

Blackwell's bookshop.

Library) and is entitled to receive a copy of every publication in the United Kingdom. It houses many millions of books, manuscripts and other ancient documents.

The Library plays an important part in Dexter's novel *The Wench is Dead*, for it is here that Morse's volunteer researcher Christine Greenaway, a Bodleian librarian, ferrets out information which helps the bedridden detective solve a crime more than a century old. In *Twilight of the Gods* it is from one of the Bodleian's windows that a sniper's shot fells Morse's favourite diva, Gwladys Probert, on her way to an honorary degree ceremony.

The Botanic Gardens, Oxford.

BONN SQUARE

This small open space is in central Oxford, near the entrance to the Westgate Shopping Centre. A war memorial is sited here and in *Service of All the Dead*: 19 one of the group of alcoholic tramps who gather around it notices, in passing, 'the odd surname of a young soldier killed by mutineers in Uganda in 1897: the name was Death'.

BOTANIC GARDEN, THE

Flanking the south side of the High between Rose Lane and the River Cherwell, these gardens occupy the site of the medieval Jewish cemetery. In 1621 they were established by the Earl of Danby for the growing of medicinal herbs and exotic species. Their layout is much the same today as it was in the seventeenth century.

The opening scene of *The Sins of the Fathers*, in which Jane Robson's father suffers a heart attack after imagining himself back in wartime Malaya, were shot here, as were scenes in *Death is Now My Neighbour*.

BRASENOSE COLLEGE

A college at the heart of the city, with its main gate facing the dome of James Gibbs's temple of literature, the Radcliffe Camera, in Radcliffe Square. Brasenose College was founded in 1509 but its history dates back considerably further, to a hall with a distinctive door-knocker in the shape of a brass nose. At some point carried by a group of dissident students to Stamford in Lincolnshire (which happens to have been where Morse grew up), the knocker returned to Brasenose College in 1890 and can now be inspected in the Dining Hall. Two Brasenose men with whom Morse would have felt quite comfortable were old Elias Ashmole, a quintessential Oxford figure who founded the ASHMOLEAN MUSEUM, and Robert Burton, author of *The Anatomy of Melancholy*, a work that might have been written for the Chief Inspector – and which he actually reads in hospital in *The Daughters of Cain*: 29. A nineteenth-century Fellow of the college was Walter Pater, the aesthete who described the *Mona Lisa* in his famous essay on Leonardo da Vinci as 'one who has the learned secrets of the grave'. Morse too might have claims to know some of those.

BRYN, MAXIMILIAN THEODORE SIEGFRIED DE

The PATHOLOGIST with whom Morse gets along best is the irascible 'hump-backed' Max, who appears in most of the novels up to and including *The Way Through the Woods*. In the first seven films he is played with sublime authority by Peter Woodthorpe.

Brasenose College.

Max is a 'world authority on VD' but 'blood, that was his speciality, really'. Other pathologists are virtually detectives in their own right, becoming involved in solving the crime at all levels. Not Max. He sticks firmly to his scientific objectivity, for, as Dexter writes in *The Dead of Jericho*: 9, 'He had a profound distrust of all such intangible notions of "responsibility", "motive", and "guilt"; and as a man he had little or no respect for the work of the police force.'

There is something almost Jacobean about Max's character. His language is direct but rich, dwelling much on food – ' "I spy a boiled shirt. You've had dinner I see. I have not," ' (*The Settling of the Sun*) and, ' "He didn't swallow anything after tea. He died before he dined" ' (*The Wolvercote Tongue*). He admits to loving blood (' "Always turned me on, blood did, even as a boy" ') and is frank about his fascination with death:

> Morse had known only one person who positively relished discussing the topic – Max, the police pathologist, who in a macabre kind of way had almost made a friend of Death. But Death had made no reciprocal arrangement and Max was police pathologist no more. (*The Daughters of Cain*: 34)

Max's coronary thrombosis, described in *The Way Through the Woods*: 32, is a hard blow for Morse. In spite of the scientist's contempt for the police, he is the nearest thing Morse has to a close friend and the two men are in some respects very much alike – enthusiastic drinkers who indulge in a good deal of light-hearted verbal sparring and share occasional melancholic confidences, as, for instance, in *The Secret of Annexe* 3:11 where they ruminate on life and death unusually over a Gin-and-Campari. After Max dies, Morse weeps when he hears the news, quoting what sounds like a line of verse but is in fact from Chapter 47 of Dickens's *Bleak House*: 'The cart is shaken all to pieces and the rugged road is very near its end.'

'BURGLAR, THE' (short story, 1994)

Seventy-five-year-old Bill Robinson is away on holiday when his equally elderly neighbour reports seeing a man acting suspiciously in front of his house. On the strength of a slight acquaintance with Robinson, Morse accompanies Lewis on the investigation.

Finding a neatly removed pane of glass in the French window, Morse pronounces fingerprinting a waste of time: 'We're dealing with a professional here. Somebody as organized as that isn't going to leave his signature.'

Morse is right about the fingerprinting but, despite the chaos of Robinson's apparently ransacked bedroom, wrong about everything else, as they discover when the victim himself returns.

This brief tale – an exercise in humorous irony rather than a crime story – was published in 1994 in *You* magazine and broadcast on BBC Radio in September 1995, read by John Turner. It was republished in *The Orion Book of Murder*, edited by Peter Haining (1996) – not very appropriately, since this mystery is entirely murder-free.

· C ·

CANAL, THE OXFORD

A map of the Oxford Canal, which runs north from Oxford to Coventry, is included in *The Wench is Dead*, a story in which Morse is preoccupied with events on the canal in the mid-nineteenth century. One of the earliest canals to have been dug in southern England, it connects Banbury, Oxford and the Thames waterway with the Warwickshire coalfield, running for seventy-seven miles through forty-three locks. Nowadays it is a purely recreational canal, though it turned a profit as a commercial waterway well into this century.

In *The Riddle of the Third Mile* – and its film equivalent, *The Last Enemy* – the body of an Oxford don turns up in the canal at Thrupp. The canal also runs past JERICHO, although it plays no significant part in *The Dead of Jericho* except in so far as Anne Scott/Staveley lives in Canal Reach.

The Oxford Canal in 1851. On the left is the Boatman's Chapel, mentioned in Dexter's The Wench is Dead:*18.*

CAR, MORSE'S

Morse's identification with his car is established in the first scene of the first film. Posing as a customer at a dishonest garage raided by his colleagues, the car is rammed and its bodywork severely dented when he drives it into the path of the escaping villain. Without his car, Morse is edgy: 'I can't think in those other cars,' he says.

In the first editions of Dexter's novels, Morse's car was a classic Lancia. But the Jaguar MK II 2.4 (registration number 248 RPA) that has been used since the beginning of the television series became so identified with Morse that, for new editions of the earlier novels, the Lancia has been changed to a Jaguar. According to Dexter, this is the only detail in the books he has felt any need to change since the beginning of Morse's television fame.

One of the great features for Morse about this car is that it originates in the 1950s, the era he looks back to for all his core values. Thus it is 'pre-electrics', as we hear in the following exchange with his garage man in *Driven to Distraction*:

GEORGE: Mind you, in my opinion it's good money after bad. Because the whole electrics is up the spout for a kick-off.

A classical statue admires a classic car: an early advertisement tailor-made to catch Morse, the classicist.

Sculptured grace......

and a special kind of motoring

which no other car in the world can offer

JAGUAR

The original die-cast model of Morse's car has appreciated tenfold in value, but the colour of the upholstery was wrong.

MORSE: What d'you mean? This car's *pre*-electrics. That's why I love it. I don't hold with electrics.

GEORGE: Just don't say I never told you.

The Jaguar Mark II – a 'compact' four-door saloon introduced in October 1959 and made until 1967 – was an enormously successful car in its day. Morse's 2.4-litre model (there were also 3.4- and 3.8-litre engine sizes) has a twin overhead cam 6-cylinder 2,483cc engine, giving 120 bhp. It is (or should be) capable of accelerating from 0–60 in 17.3 seconds, up to a maximum speed of 96.3 m.p.h. In all, there were 25,070 of this variation made out of a total output of 83,800 Mark IIs. The interior had leather-upholstered seats and walnut veneers. In the early 1960s, when Morse was still a young policeman, the car was extremely popular as a police vehicle and this was no doubt his first introduction to it. Its original retail price was £1,534.

A scale model of the Morse car in its maroon livery, produced by Corgi Classic toys, has been one of the company's most popular models. Launched in 1993 at £8.99, it now changes hands for as much as £75. A second issue, with a more accurate interior, was released in 1998.

'CARPET-BAGGER, THE' (short story, 1993)

Morse has only a walk-on part in this story of a cold and destitute van thief who, when arrested, manages to pass himself off as a harmless escaped prisoner, obtaining an overnight cell and breakfast from the Bicester Police before effecting an easy escape. Ahead of the two shamefaced arresting officers in the cafeteria queue, Morse supplies the answer to their speculations as to why the culprit, Samuel Lambert, should have been nicknamed 'Danny': ' "Might be someone from Stamford in Lincolnshire," ' Morse tells them. ' "Lamberts there often get called Danny, after Daniel Lambert – fellow who weighed fifty-two odd stone – still in *The Guinness Book of Records*." '

The rookie PC Watson is subsequently informed that this was the legendary Chief Inspector Morse. He has never met the celebrated detective, though he almost – but not quite – remembers that old Jaguar they had noticed the previous night in the lay-by, while looking for stolen lorries: the one in which there had been a grey-haired man and a 'dusky-headed young maiden' who, when she saw the officers walking past, had hurriedly refastened the buttons of her blouse.

CHAMPKIN, PETER

Author of *The Sleeping Life of Aspern Williams*, from which three of Dexter's most enigmatic chapter EPIGRAPHS are taken: *The Daughters of Cain*: 41 and 52, and *The Way Through the Woods*: 23. One might be forgiven for suspecting that this writer is from the same mould as Diogenes SMALL, but Champkin, though obscure, is real enough.

CHAUCER ROAD

There is no such road in Oxford – although there is in Cambridge – but Dexter's fictional site for the FOREIGN EXAMINATIONS SYNDICATE (*The Silent World of Nicholas Quinn*: 2) is described as one of those Victorian streets in North Oxford which link the Woodstock and the Banbury roads.

In the short story 'The Burglar' Morse and Lewis investigate a break-in at Chaucer Crescent, which is perhaps near by.

CHERUBIM AND SERAPHIM (TV film only)

This original story by SCRIPTWRITER Julian Mitchell supplies much information about Morse's childhood and his dysfunctional family background. Pitted against a corrupt scientist, he is driven on by a tragic personal bereavement.

There has been a rash of teenage suicides in the Oxford area at the same time as an experimental rave drug called Seraphim is in circulation, originally developed by an ambitious scientist, Desmond Collier, for its anti-ageing effects on geriatric patients. But how these drugs are getting on to the rave scene neither the drugs squad nor anybody else can tell Morse.

A night-time scene from Cherubim and Seraphim *is almost ready for shooting.*

Seraphim is a scourge which doubly affects him. First, his senile old step-mother is prescribed the drug and begins to recover her memory – including, among other things, how much she always hated Morse. Second, Marilyn Garrett, one of the teenage suicides, was the child of Morse's only sister, Joyce.

In vengeful pursuit of the drug dealers he believes killed his niece, Morse's grief is compounded by bruised vanity. No longer the great detective, he feels flat-footed and helpless in the face of the complexities of modern teenage life. The designer DRUGS common in this unfamiliar world of the rave scene are much more difficult for him to accept than the traditional recreations (adultery, beer) of his own generation.

As Morse says, 'On this case, Lewis, if it is a case, I feel I don't know anything at all.' The clues come together in the end, when he discovers that Collier has been deliberately using rave parties as an unofficial testing ground for his pills. However, they are leading him to the paradoxical and unwelcome finding that this wonder drug makes its users so happy that they want to die.

In many ways the mood of this film is deeply sombre and pessimistic, but Mitchell and Boyle successfully weave through it a few strands of comedy, especially in the figure of the pompous, about-to-retire Chief Inspector Holroyd. After years of Morse's eccentricities, Superintendent STRANGE thinks Lewis will benefit from a taste of the stickler Holroyd's by-the-book approach and teams them up together, while Morse, pretending to take compassionate leave, is investigating the death of the niece who was so special to him.

Morse's grief is as raw at the end as it was on the day he heard the news. But in part it is grief for his own childhood, its pains, disappointments and unfulfilled dreams.

First transmission 15 April 1992
Writer Julian Mitchell
Director Danny Boyle (*see note under* SCRIPTWRITERS)
Cast includes Isla Blair, Sorcha Cusack, Jason Isaacs, John Junkin

CHILDHOOD AND CHILDREN

Children play very little part in Morse's world and he has as little to do with them as possible. Although he may once or twice sit down to watch cartoons on TV with Lewis's kids, he has scant sympathy for or interest in his sergeant's heroic attempts to defy his own and the job's demands by staying in touch with the development of his two offspring.

'I can't imagine you young, Morse,' says Superintendent STRANGE in *Cherubim and Seraphim*. Indeed, very little, except what is revealed in this highly personal film, is known about the early years of E. Morse, at least prior to the age of fifteen. He gives the impression of having deliberately suppressed the memories, which are stirred only when the one child he, as an adult, has ever cared for, his niece Marilyn Garrett, is dead. *Cherubim and Seraphim* is the one source of concrete details about Morse's childhood and they do at least explain why he prefers not to dwell on the subject. He was the extremely unhappy child of parents who did not get on and divorced when he was twelve. About his mother, who did not, he says, 'have a fancy man', Morse expresses his feelings only once and then with revealing brevity, for it is a painful subject. In *Service of All the Dead*, Mrs Rawlinson asks him about her, to which his only reply is that she was 'loving and kind. I often think of her.'

But she died when Morse was fifteen, and he had to live with his father and the step-mother he detested. The feeling was obviously mutual. In *Cherubim and Seraphim*, when the senile Gwen Morse starts to regain her faculties under the influence of Dr Collier's wonder drug, virtually the first thing she remembers is her loathing of Morse. Morse's detestation of Gwen had one significant advantage, however. As he explained to Lewis, 'I only read poetry to annoy her. "What's this rubbish?" she'd say. I owe all the things that I love to the fact that she couldn't stand me.'

Children are occasionally in evidence in the *Morse* films. On two occasions a young daughter is used to play up the sense of pathos when one of her parents turns out to be a

The tragedy which strikes Morse's half-sister, Joyce (seen here with Morse's geriatric step-mother, Gwen) leads to revelations about Morse's own painful childhood.

murderer. In *The Settling of the Sun* we are left at the end contemplating the enormity of Alex Robson's task in coming to terms with the fact that her father is a murderer who also got himself murdered – and that her aunt, too, is a murderess. Morse rather lamely tries to comfort her but hasn't the faintest idea of how to go about it. The ending of *The Ghost in the Machine* is a less sentimental take on a similar situation. As Lady Hanbury is driven away to the police station, her six-year-old daughter, Georgina, is comforted by a woman police constable:

WPC: Now there, Georgie, you'll see her again soon.

GEORGIE: How dare you call me Georgie? My name's Georgina and I hate you.

It is clear from this that the young Georgina will have a hard time of it, but that she will pretend to be impervious, hiding behind the protective shield of wealth and class that has surrounded her thus far.

CHRIST CHURCH

This Oxford college is never referred to familiarly as a 'college' but as 'the House' – which is the sort of insider's information which the *parvenu* Paul Eirl is proud to trot out in *Who Killed Harry Field?* Founded in 1525 by Cardinal Wolsey and once called Cardinal College, it is the basis for Wolsey College in *The Daughters of Cain*, with which it shares the important eccentricity (important in the sense that it is a clue in the novel *The Daughters of Cain*) that the dons are called Students rather than Fellows. Students, in the normal sense, are called 'gentlemen of the House'.

Filming for scenes in *The Daughters of Cain*, *Last Seen Wearing* and *The Secret of Bay 5B* was carried out around Christ Church.

Porters at 'the House'.

CLASS

Morse's head is egalitarian but in his heart he is prejudiced against those of poor EDUCATION in general and imprecise users of the ENGLISH LANGUAGE in particular, making him unsympathetic to popular CULTURE in most of its forms. But if he appears to be an intellectual snob, Morse never shows a trace of social snobbery.

He and Lewis often find themselves investigating the upper echelons of society, on whom Morse wastes little sympathy. In *Last Seen Wearing* (TV film), visiting an expensive private girls' school, he remarks, 'Cream of the country, eh? . . . Rich and thick.' In *The Ghost in the Machine* he is repelled by the insensitivity of the upper class and 'all this aristocratic flummery', so he finds no difficulty at all in seeing Lady Hanbury, for example, as a murderer: 'You live in a place like this, you think the rules don't apply', and, 'People like them, they think people like us are only here to keep the servants in order.'

It is privilege above all else that Morse hates. Even in death the socially prominent get all the attention. In *Happy Families* – a public-relations disaster for Morse – the press's obsessive interest in the rich and famous infuriates him: 'Half of them wouldn't be here if it was some old lady hit on the head in her council flat.'

It is ironic, then, that in this case he himself becomes the tabloids' target as a dilettante and out-of-touch 'gentleman copper' who makes little progress in the inquiries into the murders of the Balcombe family, although he 'can still find time to indulge his passion for books, music and fine wines'. Meanwhile, he lets his 'sergeant take the strain'. Morse is incandescent with rage: 'Is it wrong to like books? To like music? They make them sound like vices. Worse . . . like the pastimes of someone foolish. And it was ten o'clock at night. In my own home!'

Morse has fallen victim to the gutter press's tendency to conflate social snobbery with CULTURE and there is nothing he can do about it – except catch the killer.

CLASSICS

Morse trained as a classicist and, although he never took his degree, many parts of his world overlap with that of the ancient Greeks and Romans.

> MORSE: You should try the myths some time, Lewis. Sex is never simple there. There's pleasure, then there's payment. Retribution.
> LEWIS: As my mother always used to say, 'Laughing always comes to crying.'

These lines come almost at the end of *Greeks Bearing Gifts*, a story in which many of the threads of tragedy, applicable both to modern and to ancient Greece, are drawn fatally together. Classical scholar Randall Rees and his wife, Friday, are cursed by barrenness; a Greek waitress gives birth to a shameful illegitimate child; and an ambitious English businessman vies with a more powerful Greek one. From these beginnings a great deal of evil and much retribution proceed.

The Dead of Jericho (both the novel and the film) shows the extent to which Morse's thinking is influenced by the powerful tradition of classical myth and legend. Looking into Anne Scott/Staveley's death, he constructs a hypothesis that 'Sophocles did it' – in other words, she became convinced that all the essential elements in the Greek playwright's tragedy *Oedipus Rex* had been replicated in her own life and that (like Oedipus's queen, Jocasta) she therefore had to kill herself. As it turns out, Morse is wrong, but it is typical of him that the theory grips him like a vice while it lasts.

While ARISTOTLE is a major influence on Morse and is constantly referred to throughout the novels, there are also important references to other classical figures. To take one example, the Roman poet Gaius Valerius Catullus (*c.* 84 – *c.* 54 BC) is a strong presence in *The Daughters of Cain*, in which Morse discovers that the emotions and imagination of the murder victim, Dr Felix McClure, had been stirred by Catullus's erotic poetry – as indeed his own had once been. In particular, while searching McClure's flat he stumbles on the dead man's translation of poem 58, a verse about a refined woman who likes to play the public whore, thereby arousing the poet's passionate jealousy. The poem suddenly evokes memories of Morse's own sexual jealousy from more than thirty years ago when, at the age of eighteen, his girlfriend had betrayed him with another man: 'Jealousy, the most corrosive of all the emotions, gnawing away at the heart with greater pain than failure or hatred – or even despair.'

And then there is Homer.

> If, for him, the whole of the Classical corpus had to be jettisoned except for one single passage, he would probably have opted for the scene depicting the death of Sarpedon, from Book XVI of *The Iliad*, where those swift companions, the twin brothers Sleep and Death, bear the dead hero to the pleasant land of Lycia. (*The Daughters of Cain*: 44)

An engraving of the death of Sarpedon, Morse's favourite episode from The Iliad.

This passage is referred to again in *The Way Through the Woods*: 37. What is its significance for Morse? As balm, perhaps, to the troubled spirit of a man with no fixed RELIGION, PHOBIAS about corpses and the dark and a generally morbid temperament.

Many of the Morse films follow classical conventions, not so much of structure but of motive and situation. Morse himself sees this at the end of *The Last Enemy*, as they contemplate the wicked deeds of the don who happens to have once been Morse's classics tutor:

> LEWIS: His disease has turned him into a madman.
> MORSE: It's in the best classical tradition, Lewis. The man of virtue puts right the wrongs that have been done to him . . .

The Infernal Serpent is perhaps the most classically 'tragic' of all the *Morse* films. Here the Master of Beaufort is killed – *has* to be killed – because he is the source of a corruption which spreads right through the family and the college. His wife says afterwards, 'There was a serpent in our house, coiled around the foundations.' Here the 'house' can be understood in a number of ways – as a building, a college or, in the way that a Greek tragedian would speak of the accursed 'House of Atreus', a family that is blighted by the evil embedded at its core.

CODE(S)

Codes and coded letters are a delight to Morse, the inveterate lover of CROSSWORDS. He discovers in *Last Bus to Woodstock* the mis-spelt letter received by Jennifer Coleby at her work which seems to refer to a job application she never made. But later that evening, as he tackles a fiendish crossword in which 'each of the across clues contains a deliberate misprint', Morse realizes that the same is true for almost every line of the Coleby letter. The added or subtracted letters spell out a message: 'SAY NOTHING'. In the film, the message is changed, because now it accompanies a large sum of money and reads 'PLEASE TAKE IT'.

Another coded letter turns up in *The Silent World of Nicholas Quinn*: 8. This time, the last words in each line make up the concealed message: 'YOUR PACKAGE READY FRIDAY 21ST ROOM THREE. PLEASE DESTROY THIS IMMEDIATELY.'

In *The Riddle of the Third Mile*, Morse is presented with the negative of this problem, a letter cut in half vertically so that the right-hand part is missing. He rises to the challenge joyfully, reconstructing the missing words from the known context, mixed with some inspired guesswork, with all the relish of a biblical archaeologist piecing together a Dead Sea scroll.

The short story 'The Inside Story' presents a slightly different kind of corrupted text. Here the murder victim, Sheila Poster (under the name Elissa Thorpe), has entered a crime-writing competition to be judged by one Rex de Lincto, Chairman of the Oxford Book Association. Morse has reason to believe the story she has written is, in some of its elements, a true guide to what happened to her, but the problem is to sort the wheat of fact from the chaff of fiction. Again, he throws himself into the task with gusto.

Although he perhaps misses the incidental opportunity to decode the identity of 'Rex de Lincto' in 'The Inside Story', Morse cracks many rather more useful anagrammatical clues in the course of his work. In *Service of All the Dead* the tramp Swanpole's identity is discovered when Morse realizes the name is an anagram of 'P. E. Lawson', the Reverend Lawson's brother. (In the TV versions he is 'S. O. Pawlen'). In *The Wench is Dead*, the name Don Favant suddenly resolves itself into F. T. Donavan and, again, all is clear. Morse knows where he is when dealing with like-minded (for which read 'crossword-minded') villains, but his cryptogrammatic brain can sometimes lead him astray. In *The Riddle of the Third Mile*, the identity of a disappearing fisherman, 'Simon Rowbotham', whom Morse is anxious to interview, seems to point anagrammatically to Morse's old classics tutor, O. M. A. Browne-Smith, and it takes Lewis to spot that for a true anagram the 'e' should have been an 'o'.

Finally, in the film *Absolute Conviction* the identity of an innocent-looking but villainous crossword-puzzler is revealed because, though his real name is Harold Manners, he has adopted the pseudonym Roland Sherman – a simple anagram to a man of Morse's capability.

COINCIDENCE

Lewis's perennial scepticism about Morse's more far-flung fancies often begins when he spots an unlikely coincidence: 'Don't you think it's a bit of a coincidence that you and this Gilbert fellow should have a bad tooth at the same time?'

Morse enjoys these exchanges because they give him the opening he needs to mount one of his hobby horses:

> Coincidences are far more commonplace than any of us are willing to accept . . . And, if you must go on about coincidence, you just go home tonight and find the forty-sixth word from the beginning of the forty-sixth psalm, and the forty-sixth word from the end of it – and see what you land up with! Authorized Version, by the way. (*The Riddle of the Third Mile*: 19)

(If Lewis had carried out Morse's instructions, he would have found the first of these words is 'shake' and the second is 'spear'.)

CORPSES

For a CID man who is rarely either happy or particularly useful except when investigating a murder, Morse has a curious handicap: a horror of dead bodies. On several occasions he is sick after viewing a corpse; on others he retreats into flippancy. In *Last Bus to Woodstock*: 2, the first novel, he is 'more interested in the starry heavens above' than in examining the body of a murdered girl. In *Driven to Distraction*, arriving at the murder scene he passes a remark that makes the scene-of-crime officers laugh – much to the distress of the corpse's boyfriend, who overhears from the next room. Morse tries to explain: 'It, er, wasn't a joke. Not that it makes any difference. But I . . . you have to find a way to deal with these things, that's all. I'm sorry.'

About the true nature of this condition, however, Morse is not always quite sure. In *The Daughters of Cain*: 55 we find him musing on it:

> Morse was not really afraid of dead bodies at all, or so he told himself. What he really suffered from was a completely new form of phobia, one that was all his own: *the fear of being sick* at the sight of bodies which had met their deaths in strange or terrible circumstances. Even Morse, for all his classical education, was unable to coin an appropriately descriptive, or etymologically accurate, term for such a phobia.

See also PHOBIAS, MORSE'S.

COURTENAY COLLEGE

The fictional college of which the aristocratic former diplomat Sir Julius Hanbury in *The Ghost in the Machine* is the murdered head.

CRICKET

Morse has always disliked SPORT, according to Colin Dexter. Yet in *Last Seen Wearing*: 5, 'Morse still kept his batting averages somewhere', and in *Service of All the Dead*: 12 there is enough of the game in his subconscious to allow a cricket analogy to drift into his talk with old Mrs Rawlinson. Something has clearly happened to destroy his illusions about the game. In *Deceived by Flight* (the film plotted by Colin Dexter), he is openly bored at a match in which Lewis – an enthusiast – is playing with some success: 'Men in uniforms, incomprehensible rules, nothing happening for hours, everyone taking it very seriously. Not my idea of a good time.'

The team in *Deceived by Flight* is a loose association of chums, the Clarets, who get together once a year for a short tour, starting in Oxford and moving on to play in Holland. This type of outfit, playing in parks and on village greens against all sorts of local sides, is the mainstay of the amateur game as it has been played in England every summer for centuries. Its descent in this story into a cover for drug smuggling is a typical motif in *Morse*, an index of the decline in English national life since the 1950s, which is one of Morse's most consistent preoccupations.

Village cricket in the 1950s – a scene from Morse's irrecoverably lost world.

CROSSWORD(S)

It is no accident that Morse shares his name with one of the greatest of all crossword brains, the banker Sir Jeremy Morse. Crosswords play a vital part in the Chief Inspector's life: they are his favourite mental exercise, a form of cerebral jogging which he regards as essential to the well-being of his brain. His dedication or addiction to the crossword – by which he means, of course, the *cryptic* crossword – appears almost as soon as he is introduced in the first novels. Here, in *Last Bus to Woodstock*: 2, Lewis and the subordinate constables are busy until almost midnight taking a mountain of statements from the customers in the Black Prince pub. Not Morse. After a cursory glance at the car park, where the body was found, he repairs to the publican's office where Lewis is rather shocked to find him drinking 'what looked very much like whisky' and immersed in the back of *The Times*:

> 'Ah, Lewis.' He thrust the paper across. 'Have a look at 14 down. Appropriate eh?'
> Lewis looked at 14 down: *Take in bachelor? It could do* (3). He saw what Morse had written into the completed diagram: BRA. What was he supposed to say? He had never worked with Morse before.

From here on, at various time, crossword puzzles crop up regularly in the novels and films. Morse is sometimes so caught up in a crossword that he will send Lewis off to carry out some door-to-door inquiries while he 'catches up with some paperwork' – which means in reality he has Sunday's Ximenes to complete. In crossword terms *The Times* is his daily bread, normally taking him ten minutes to finish (he invariably times himself), although there is often one clue he cannot crack: in *The Silent Word of Nicholas Quinn*: 20 the recalcitrant one is, 'In which are the Islets of Langerhans' (8). It takes Morse several more precious minutes to come up with the answer: *pancreas*.

In *Last Bus to Woodstock*: 9, the instructions for one of the most difficult of all crosswords, in the now-defunct *Listener* weekly, provide him with a vital clue for tackling the otherwise inexplicable letter sent to his suspect, Jennifer Coleby (see CODE(S)).

Sometimes the crossword gives him a psychological lift, as when, on a day from which he expects much, he finds 1 across to be: '*Code name for a walrus* (5). Ha! The clue was like a megaphone shouting the answer to him. It was going to be his day.' (Last Seen Wearing: 16)

And there are suggestions here and there that crossword-puzzlers are a kind of community, a freemasonry. In the film of *The Silent World of Nicholas Quinn* Morse finds to his delight that suspect, and later murder victim, Philip Ogleby, is a crossword setter, which immediately creates a bond between them.

A psychoanalyst might say that Morse's interest in infuriating, absorbing verbal puzzles is a function of his yearning to understand the seemingly inexplicable and his need to fill in the emotional voids in his life. The more prosaic explanation concerns his creator Colin Dexter's own prowess as a cruciverbalist, which is a matter of record. Dexter has five times been national champion of the *Observer's* fiendish Ximenes/Azed puzzles and, in Don Manley's *Chambers' Crossword Manual* (1986), is given equal billing to the man Dexter lauded when he named his detective: 'Over the past thirty years, N. C. Dexter has probably been the most brilliant clue-writer, but C. J. Morse has been the most consistent.'

CULTURE

When Lewis makes a reference to Morse on HOLIDAY lying on a beach, the Chief Inspector testily replies, 'I spent my holiday in cultural pursuits, Lewis, *not* lying on a beach.' (*Deadly Slumber*)

Overall, Morse regards himself as a man of high cultural standards. However, this is not the whole story. In the prologue to *Death is Now My Neighbour*, his answers to the questionnaire in the *Police Gazette* testing readers' levels of culture contain some surprises, such as a preference for Kim Basinger over Princess Diana and Mother Teresa and the video *Copenhagen Red Hot Sex 2* over *Casablanca*.

See also CLASS, CLASSICS, LITERATURE, MUSIC.

· D ·

DAUGHTERS OF CAIN, THE (novel, 1994)

At WOLSEY COLLEGE, dons are known formally as students, a potentially confusing fact which puts everyone except Morse on the wrong scent during the police investigation into the death of Dr Felix McClure, a retired classics Fellow found stabbed in his book-lined flat. McClure had previously incurred the enmity of a college scout, Edward Brooks, by having the man sacked, although the reader will waste little sympathy on Brooks since he is a wife-beating, child-abusing drug dealer. Before and after his retirement, McClure had also been besotted by Brooks's step-daughter, Ellie Smith, a prostitute whom he beguiled by translating the erotic Latin poetry of Catullus. Interested in Catullus and, like Prime Minister Gladstone, always fascinated by prostitutes, Morse finds it a pleasant duty to question the girl, though, with her ringed nostrils and scarlet-streaked hair, she simultaneously attracts and repels him.

Poles apart, but drifting into flirtation. Morse and Kay Brooks on the river in The Daughters of Cain.

There are many potential distractions in this case, not least a threatened breakdown in HEALTH which lands Morse in the JOHN RADCLIFFE HOSPITAL for tests. Investigations of a (to him) more welcome kind must also be made at the PITT-RIVERS MUSEUM, where, having left Wolsey College, Brooks has been working as a guard. There is much to interest Morse here. He notices with a *frisson* that the museum has a large collection of shrunken heads and many other artefacts of an exotic and murderous nature. At the same time Jane Cotterell, the museum's administrator, is an attractive and intelligent forty-something woman . . .

Another diversion is Julia Stevens, the equally attractive, Titian-haired teacher from the Proctor Memorial School, who employs Brooks's wife, Brenda, as a cleaner. Or *is* she such a diversion? The more Morse thinks about her, the larger Mrs Stevens looms in his inquiries, especially after Brooks himself goes missing, presumed murdered. Julia Stevens, Ellie Smith, Brenda Brooks: a trio of suspects, the three 'daughters of Cain'.

DAUGHTERS OF CAIN, THE (TV film)

Julian Mitchell's adaptation parallels Dexter's novel, although there is an important difference in the character of Ellie (now Kay). Instead of being a punkish, low-grade prostitute, she becomes a high-class call girl established in London – a change which naturally increases her allure for Morse.

First transmission 22 November 1996
Writer Julian Mitchell
Director Herbert Wise
Cast includes Tony Haygarth, Gabrielle Lloyd, Phyllis Logan, Amanda Ryan, Benjamin Whitrow

DAY OF THE DEVIL, THE (TV film only)

Sceptical enough whenever he is dealing with orthodox RELIGION, Morse here confronts the inversion of Christian belief: Satanism. He consults a clerical expert on the subject, Canon Appleton, who explains the devil's morality:

> 'Foul is fair and fair is foul, Chief Inspector. That's what your satanic Bible amounts to. Righteousness is but a fetter on man. Remove it and you have the Superman . . . The occult will always be with us, Chief Inspector. It reflects a part of our nature.'

Dismissive of this at first, it is a shock to Morse's system to discover that Appleton is right and that Satanism is actually a working religion. It is even more shattering to his notions of fitness and rationality to find later that there are Oxford University men among the paid-up members.

But is prison escapee and self-styled Satanist John Peter Barrie a sincere believer – or just posing as one of the coven? Morse sticks to his view that Barrie is no more than a common rapist, psychopath and con man, though his behaviour is puzzling all the same. Instead of running away, Barrie lingers in the Oxford area. His first move is to kidnap a

Foul is fair: Morse discovers that Satanism is a working religion.

local woman and demand that his prison psychiatrist, Esther Martin, be brought to see him (he apparently believes that Dr Martin is one of Satan's handmaidens).

Charmed himself by the attractive Dr Martin, Morse is led a not-so-merry dance by Barrie, who always seems to be 'one step ahead' of his pursuers. Convinced that he is receiving help, Lewis and Morse stumble upon a satanic coven whose members include the Bursar of LONSDALE COLLEGE himself.

In a piece of bravura film-making, the group is shown holding dawn rites on Lammas Day. The devil's disciples are scared witless when a ring of fire explodes around them and a figure with the head of a goat and the body of a man walks towards them through the flames to deal out satanic retribution.

But for Morse the most troubling question of all is whether Esther Martin is herself part of the cult. And why exactly does Barrie want to join up with her? Morse is uncharacteristically slow in getting to the answers and the result, far from being a routine and tidy arrest, is a bloody showdown in a quiet Oxford suburb.

First transmission 13 January 1993
Writer Daniel Boyle
Director Stephen Whittaker
Cast includes Keith Allen, Richard Griffiths, Harriet Walter and the voice of Janis Kelly singing Massenet

'DEAD AS A DODO' (short story, 1991)

Morse gives Philip Wise, one of his North Oxford neighbours, a lift up the traffic-choked Banbury Road one night and is treated to the story of Wise's youthful friendship with Dodo Whitaker, a mysterious boiler-suited girl whom he met in wartime Oxford, and her brother Ambrose, who became his drinking companion. Although he had lost touch with the Whitakers before the war ended, Philip had recently seen an announcement for the funeral service of Ambrose Whitaker and, out of curiosity, had attended, hoping to see Dodo again. In fact, the sister he meets is nothing like Dodo yet, he is told, this is the only sister Ambrose had. So who was Dodo? Morse quickly disposes of Philip's own theory – that Dodo was really Ambrose's secret wife – and sets out to test a hypothesis of his own with a call to the Ministry of Defence. Needless to say, he is right . . .

DEADLY SLUMBER (TV film only)

Matthew Brewster is murdered in the garage of his own home – bound and gagged inside his car with the engine running and the doors locked. Could his son, John, have done it to protect his sick mother from Brewster's infidelities? Or is the murderer bookmaker Michael Steppings, whose daughter, Avril, is lying in a coma after a botched and negligent minor operation at the Brewsters' private clinic? Once Morse discovers that Steppings had sent the Brewsters a series of threatening letters, the bookmaker's arrest is inevitable.

Inevitable, but a mistake, for Morse can't shake Steppings's alibi and has to release him. Then John Brewster confesses that *he* killed his father and the case seems to be over. But Morse is still not satisfied and so the familiar pattern is repeated, with Morse reaching the truth via a process of persistently arresting the wrong people. Once he realizes that there is, apart from his son and Steppings, another person with a deadly grudge against Matthew Brewster, and that this person is in league with Steppings, then the path to the truth is cleared.

In this film, Morse presents an unusually mellow face to the world. His whole demeanour is determined by the fact that he can't help but like Michael Steppings. And he is enormously impressed by the fact that Steppings visits his daughter in hospital every day of his life, doggedly reading novels and stories to her though she shows no sign of hearing or knowing that he is there. Morse is so touched by this that he makes sure daily flowers are sent to Avril Steppings's room while her father is in custody. Even when Steppings later offers him an enormous bribe – something that would normally have Morse bristling like a porcupine – he merely returns the cheque:

MORSE: I can't accept this.
STEPPINGS: You could go anywhere . . .
MORSE: Yes, but what would I do when I got there?

Morse's ever-present concern for justice is only half satisfied by the outcome of this film. The greedy, cost-cutting Brewsters are destroyed, but what about Steppings? 'He was monstrous,' says John Brewster. In other cases and at other times Morse might have gone along with such an idea. In *The Day of the Devil*, for instance, the film which followed this one, and was also written by Daniel Boyle, there is nothing to be said in mitigation of the criminal. John Peter Barrie really is monstrous, whereas here Morse hints at his sympathy for a more liberal, *Guardian*-reading theory of the roots of evil: 'Was he, Mr Brewster? Your parents and Nurse Hazlitt ruined his daughter's life, and for no other reason than to save money . . . If Michael Steppings was monstrous, Mr Brewster, he was made monstrous.'

First transmission 6 January 1993
Writer Daniel Boyle
Director Stuart Orme
Cast includes Brian Cox, Penny Downie, Jason Durr, Janet Suzman

DEAD OF JERICHO, THE (novel, 1981)

> He was fifty and age was just about beginning, so he told himself, to cure his heart of tenderness. Just about. (1)

Some hope . . . Morse is not even fooling himself. With his weakness for women in their thirties, he spends the first few pages of the novel falling for languages home-tutor Anne Scott at a party. It is, of course, a fatal attraction. Mistakenly thinking Anne is married, Morse doesn't contact her again until months later when, on his way to deliver some unwanted paperbacks to a second-hand book sale, he impulsively calls at her house in the Oxford district of JERICHO. There is no reply, but, if she is out why is the door unlocked and why does he get the feeling that there is someone at home? After hesitating for a moment in the hallway, Morse turns and quietly leaves.

Later that evening, an anonymous phone call directs the police to Anne Scott's house, where she is found dead, having apparently hanged herself. Morse's first task is to establish the reason for her death, whether it was murder or suicide. The pathology report reveals that she had been pregnant, and the police start by considering who might be the father. They are shocked to discover that Morse himself would seem to be in the frame. Not only are the initials 'E.M.' – his own – pencilled into Anne Scott's diary for the day of her death, but old George Jackson, the busybody and local odd-job man across the street, had seen Morse leaving her house that afternoon.

Having overcome these minor difficulties, Morse is soon on the case, considering possible lines of approach. There are various suspects, including the philandering publisher who once employed Anne, a teenage boy who was her pupil, and Jackson. Then he finds that Anne has been reading *Oedipus Rex*, the Greek tragedy in which a mother unknowingly sleeps with her son and commits suicide. Morse begins to construct the theory that the case is, in his own words, a 'ghastly re-enactment of the old myth as you can read it in Sophocles' (33). But Morse is so mesmerized by the beauty of the most Baroque theory he ever devised, it is left to Lewis, with his implacable devotion to steady police work, to put the Chief Inspector back on the right track.

With the object of Morse's romantic dreams lying in the morgue by the end of the second chapter, there is, understandably, an even more than usually melancholic under-tone to this book. Early on in the narrative Morse attends a meeting of the Oxford Book Association, addressed by the distinguished (and perfectly genuine) scholar Professor Dame Helen Gardner. The lines she quotes from T. S. Eliot's *Four Quartets* strike a particular sombre chord with Morse:

> Footfalls echo in the memory
> Down the passage which we did not take
> Towards the door we never opened.

DEAD OF JERICHO, THE (TV film)

The very first Morse television adaptation is substantially faithful to Dexter's novel, although a number of details are tweaked to allow for differences between the print and film media. Morse meets Anne (now renamed Staveley and a piano teacher) at the Choral Society and he walks her home. His courtship, painfully diffident at the best of times, is hardly helped by the presence of a disconcerting undergraduate at her JERICHO house.

This is a budding composer who has the run of her home, her piano and maybe even her bed, while there is also in Anne's background an ex-employer/lover. But, as in the novel, it is the fact of Anne's pregnancy that leads to her death – and leads Morse to formulate his elaborate Oedipal hypothesis about the ultimate cause of that death.

Morse and Anne Staveley – another doomed romance.

First transmission 6 January 1987
Writer Anthony Minghella
Director Alastair Reid
Cast includes Gemma Jones, James Laurenson, Patrick Troughton

DEAD ON TIME (TV film only)

A figure from Morse's distant romantic past reappears in this film in the shape of the serenely beautiful Susan (Joanna David), who, as a student, had been engaged to marry Morse before giving him up in favour of an older man, the brilliant law professor Henry Fallon. But her family has been devastated by tragedy – the deaths of her daughter and small granddaughter in a car accident two years earlier and now that of her wheelchair-bound husband. Fallon's death from a neurological condition was inevitable in any case and suicide is assumed by all, until his doctor reveals that Henry Fallon's condition would have made it impossible for him to pull the trigger.

Suspicion falls on the Fallons' impecunious son-in-law, Peter Rhodes, who found the body and may have had his hopes for a loan from Professor Fallon dashed.

Increasingly rebesotted by Susan, Morse goes for Rhodes in a big way, subjecting him to a fierce interrogation, but Rhodes puts up a convincing display of innocence. Initially Morse refuses to see it, but he is finally made to realize that Fallon's death is much more complicated – a family compact of death and revenge in which Susan Fallon seems to be deeply implicated. Morse prefers to blame the family doctor, but then Susan kills herself. Arresting the doctor, Morse physically attacks him in the presence of Lewis and STRANGE accusing him of killing both Fallon and Susan. His colleagues know that these accusations, even if partly true, can never be proved.

Morse's behaviour when in love is usually hangdog or, at best, reticent and unsure. Here we see a more positive side to his romantic persona. He courts Susan Fallon not only with tact and sympathy but also with humour, and even a touch of clowning. This seems to work for him when, half-way through the third act, she spends the night with him. But when it all goes wrong, and he loses Susan again, Morse lashes out in his anguish, showing the passionate nature which has always seemed to lie submerged beneath his grouchy cynicism.

First transmission 26 February 1992
Writer Daniel Boyle
Director John Madden
Cast includes Samantha Bond, Joanna David, Adrian Dunbar, David Haig, Richard Pasco

DEATH IS NOW MY NEIGHBOUR (novel, 1996)

As on previous occasions, the plot of Dexter's most recent *Morse* novel revolves around competition between specimens of that most common life-form in the world of Morse, the Oxford don. This species is both pampered and complacent, and its members frequently appear to have more than enough time on their hands to lead them into mischief and mayhem. The retiring Master of LONSDALE COLLEGE, Sir Clixby Bream, belongs firmly in this category, a 'smooth and odious' old lecher whom Morse dislikes so much he

'You're supposed to be working!' 'I'm a detective. Detectives think, mainly. Today, I choose to do my thinking lying down.' Morse with love-of-his-life, Susan Fallon.

won't even take a drink from him. The only two candidates for the succession are the flashy anthropologist and philanderer Julian Storrs ('*Recreations*: taking taxis, playing bridge') and historian Denis Cornford. Cornford, best known for his whimsical theory that the Battle of Hastings really happened in 1065 ('*Recreations*: kite-flying, cultivation of orchids'), is a warmer, more sympathetic character than Storrs. However, there is little that his wife – as is equally true for Mrs Storrs – will stop at to secure the post for her husband, and the honorific knighthood that goes with it, including having sex with the sixty-nine-year-old but still lively Sir Clixby.

Now after the breakfast-time death of a physiotherapist named Rachel James in her KIDLINGTON home, the question before Morse is whether ambition has driven one of the four to murder. Initially he has trouble identifying a motive for why Miss James should be shot through her misted-up kitchen window. He knows she had been having an affair with Dr Storrs, but his suspicion falls first on her next-door neighbour, Geoffrey Owens, a seedy journalist who has been taking a close interest in the contest for the Lonsdale Mastership, while making furtive visits to London's Soho to interview a variety of hookers and strippers. But Morse's theories about the connection between these activities are tipped back into the melting pot when Owens himself is murdered and the Chief Inspector evolves a new theory turning on the superstitious avoidance of the number thirteen.

In his private life, Morse faces a new threat to his HEALTH when he is diagnosed as diabetic and spends an anxious few days in the JOHN RADCLIFFE HOSPITAL.

This novel is notable for at last revealing, in its final chapter, the secret of Morse's Christian name – Endeavour.

DEATH IS NOW MY NEIGHBOUR (TV film)

Mitchell's film omits any mention of Morse's diabetic illness, which plays such a prominent part in the novel. The other principal difference, in an adaptation which otherwise sticks closely to Dexter's work, is in the behaviour of Shelly Cornford (played by Holly Chant). Instead of offering herself to Sir Clixby Bream to obtain his vote in favour of her husband as Master, she is blackmailed by Bream, played by a wonderfully creepy Richard Briers in theatrically dyed-black hair:

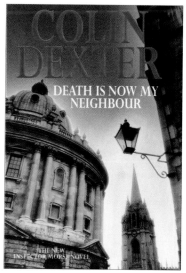

The first edition of Dexter's Death is Now My Neighbour.

> BREAM: I presently have the power to change your life. And I don't see the point in having power if one doesn't abuse it, do you?
> SHELLY: This isn't funny, Clixby.

Morse and Lewis question the manipulative Sir Clixby Bream in Death is Now My Neighbour.

BREAM: No. The deal is, as you Americans say, I can make Denis Master only if *you* . . . Think of it as charity, my dear – making an old man happy.

Gritting her teeth, Shelly goes along with the Master, only to be told afterwards that he would never vote for her husband anyway, because Cornford had once had an affair with his own wife and 'ruined my marriage. I've waited a long time for the chance to ruin his. Thank you for being so obliging.'

First transmission 19 November 1997
Writer Julian Mitchell
Director Charles Beeson
Cast includes Roger Allam, Richard Briers, Holly Chant, Judy Loe, John Shrapnel, Maggie Steed

DEATH OF THE SELF, THE (TV film only)

Morse and Lewis travel to Vicenza in Italy to investigate the fate of a popular novelist and Oxford resident, May Lawrence, who had died in an apparent accident while attending a fashionable encounter group. The organizer and guru is well known to the Thames Valley Police: Russell Clarke, 'the biggest bloody shyster on the books,' according to Superintendent STRANGE.

All is very different from the journey to New South Wales in *Promised Land*. This is the home of opera and Roman civilization, and the Chief Inspector enjoys everything about it. He gets by with enthusiastic ease in Italian and even the sound of it spoken over the Tannoy at the station, as he tells the sceptical Lewis, 'sounds like a poem to me'.

Morse and Nicole discuss death, betrayal and stage fright at Verona's Roman theatre.

Lewis, on the other hand, is at a complete loss without his *Daily Mirror* and egg and chips for supper.

The local police inspector, Battisti, is courtesy itself, though he considers the English policemen's visit a waste of time. He assents when Morse asks to be allowed to 'apply my own methods', but his patience runs thin when the Oxford detectives start digging far deeper than he thinks is required. On the other hand, Battisti doesn't see fit to tell Morse that he is himself investigating the clients and acquaintances of Russell Clarke. One of these is the playboy Italian husband of Nicole Burgess, a beautiful broken-down opera singer who has been trying to cure her stage-fright under Clarke's guidance. Naturally she becomes the irresistible magnet for Morse's ever-susceptible romantic soul.

The climax of the film is reached in the great open-air Roman theatre at Verona. As the strands of Morse and Lewis's investigation at last twine together, Burgess makes her triumphant comeback in *Turandot*, while the hopelessly besotted English policeman sits, anonymously in the huge audience, with tears streaming down his cheeks.

First transmission 25 March 1992
Writer Alma Cullen
Director Colin Gregg
Cast includes Frances Barber, Michael Kitchen and the soprano voice of Janis Kelly

DECEIVED BY FLIGHT (TV film only)

An amateur CRICKET team of old ARNOLD COLLEGE students, the Clarets, comes to Oxford led by Morse's old college chum Roland Marshall (Norman Rodway), who embarrassingly broadcasts the nickname Morse had been given at university: 'Pagan'. A much closer friend is another team member, Anthony Donn (Daniel Massey), who spends an evening with Morse. Donn is clearly troubled, but Morse fails to discover exactly why – something he regrets two days later, when Donn is murdered in his room in college.

From the first, Morse regards the murder as something to do with the team, and perhaps also Donn's wife, Kate, a successful radio presenter. Although on leave – 'I've got the outside of the house to paint and some gutters to fix and what have you' – Lewis the cricket lover cannot resist Morse's suggestion that he act as Morse's inside man, becoming an emergency replacement for Donn by posing as a Lonsdale College scout who is 'a bit useful' at the game. Morse's supposition proves partly right – but leads him into more emotional pain since he inevitably finds himself falling a little in love with the beautiful Kate Donn. The whole investigation is bedevilled by the fact that something else is going on among the Clarets and the Thames Valley Police are not the only ones taking a discreet interest in their activities. This complex entanglement of crimes rates among Colin Dexter's favourite *Morse* films.

First transmission 18 January 1989
Writer Anthony Minghella, based on an idea by Colin Dexter
Director Anthony Simmons
Cast includes Geoffrey Beevors, Jane Booker, Nicky Henson, Daniel Massey, Sharon Maughan, Stephen Moore, Bryan Pringle, Norman Rodway

DEWAR

There are two different men in the Thames Valley Police with this name. In *The Settling of the Sun* we meet Chief Superintendent Dewar of the Drugs Squad (played by Robert Lang), whom Morse detests and if possible avoids. Meanwhile, in *The Secret of Bay 5B*, there is Inspector Cyril Dewar (played by Brian Poyser), with whom Morse is on speaking terms at the Oxford TOWN HALL ball. However, he is glad enough to be rescued from this Dewar's company also when Lewis summons him to the murder in the WESTGATE CAR PARK.

DEXTER, COLIN

The creator of Morse was born, like his character, on 29 September 1930. The son of a taxi driver, he grew up in the historic Lincolnshire market town of Stamford, where he attended the local grammar school. He did his National Service in the Royal Corps of Signals, where he was, coincidentally, a Morse-Code operator, capable of speeds of 120 characters per minute. He then entered St Christ's College, Cambridge, as an undergraduate, before becoming a classics master, eventually at Corby Grammar School.

Dexter published three textbooks while a schoolmaster in collaboration with his great friend, the distinguished historian Edgar Rayner. The first was *Liberal Studies: An Outline Course, Volumes 1 and 2* (1964) – a series of essays and articles on selected topics of general interest, followed in most cases by a list of quotations taken from various sources, aimed at sixth-formers. The two authors followed this with *A Guide To Contemporary Politics* (1966), aimed at the same readership, and consisting of a series of dialogues in which speakers represent different positions on the spectrum of political views at the time. These books were published by the Pergamon Press, which was then based at Headington Hill Hall in Oxford, the home of the company's proprietor, Robert Maxwell (see note in TWILIGHT OF THE GODS).

In the mid-1960s increasing deafness forced Dexter out of teaching and he moved to Oxford to join the University of Oxford Delegacy of Local Examinations as senior assistant secretary. Here his duties included helping to set and administer public examinations for over 3,000 schools – a setting similar to the background of *The Silent World of Nicholas Quinn*.

His career as a detective-story writer began during a wet family-holiday in north Wales, when the two whodunnits in the Dexter holiday cottage proved disappointing and where he was convinced that he could do better. *Last Bus to Woodstock* was later accepted and published by Macmillan, without revisions, in 1975. Dexter writes his novels in longhand, beginning at the first chapter and going on until he reaches the end; whereupon he goes back to the beginning and rewrites the entire story a

Colin Dexter: a walk-on part in Happy Families.

second time. The method obviously works. His trophy-cabinet boasts two Silver and two Gold Daggers awarded by the Crime Writers' Association, and in 1997 he received the ultimate recognition, the Diamond Dagger for a lifetime's achievement in crime writing.

Dexter is known for appearing, Hitchcock-like, in walk-on parts in his films. He began the tradition as a passer-by in *The Dead of Jericho*, and can similarly be glimpsed somewhere in every one of the subsequent episodes. Recently he has been branching out into more ambitious roles, playing anything from a tramp drinking meths at Oxford's Carfax in *Happy Families* to a bishop in *Death is Now My Neighbour*. In two films Dexter's voice is heard: in *Deadly Slumber* he plays a library porter conducting Morse up to see young Brewster, to whom he calls like a gentle voice of doom: 'Mr Brewster!' In *Death is Now My Neighbour*, at the start of dinner in LONS-DALE COLLEGE, he is a bishop pronouncing a fairly lengthy grace at High Table.

Dexter also makes the odd appearance in his own prose fiction. In 'The Inside Story' he turns up as the anagramatic Rex de Lincto, 'the short, fat, balding, slightly deaf' Oxford Book Association chairman; and in 'Neighbourhood Watch', another short story, the physical description of Dr Eric Ullman also has much that is reminiscent: a man who lives, like Dexter, in a house with a garage on the Banbury Road, 'a small, bald-headed man with a beer belly and an NHS hearing-aid in his right ear'.

DICKSON, CONSTABLE

The cerebrally challenged, doughnut-loving Dickson is a gargantuan trencherman and frequent butt of Morse's sarcasm. He is first glimpsed in *Last Bus to Woodstock* and reappears in *Last Seen Wearing*, *The Silent World of Nicholas Quinn* and *The Riddle of the Third Mile*. By *The Jewel That Was Ours* – as 'Dixon' – he has been 'newly promoted' sergeant.

DRIVEN TO DISTRACTION (TV film only)

Most murders in Morse's casebook are killings of occasion: they come out of particular family or professional circumstances. Such murders are ideal material for a policeman who works with a puzzle-solver's intuition – he calls it 'imagination' – testing in his mind all the permutations until he reaches the solution, and thus the killer. But in this case, for the only time in the whole canon of novels and films, Morse has to confront a serial killer. This man has already killed twice and Morse is well aware that, if he cannot establish a logical connection between the victims, he stands no chance of making an arrest by his usual intuitive means. So, in an early scene, we find the Chief Inspector with his team at the incident room, throwing around ideas in an attempt to come up with such links.

The two young women have been killed by the same method but the only other con-nection the police can establish is that each of them had bought a car from the same showroom. This is run by the sleazy, womanizing Jeremy Boynton (Patrick Malahide), whom Morse takes against almost immediately. Convinced that Boynton is his man, Morse pursues him relentlessly, even to the point of harassment and breaking all the rules of POLICE PROCEDURE. There are some choice moments in Minghella's expert script. Morse's tongue is heard at its most acid, but there are several other scenes in which the comedy is at the Chief Inspector's expense – when, for example, he takes lessons at the driving school next door to Boynton's garage so he can 'pop in on a regular basis', and when he spars with the feminist Detective Sergeant Siobhan Maitland (Mary Jo Randle) drafted in as an expert on crimes against women.

In the end, Morse's usual method of 'blundering about' until he reaches the right answer lets him down. He tumbles to the real murderer only by chance – and at considerable personal risk.

First transmission 17 January 1990
Writer Anthony Minghella
Director Sandy Johnson
Cast includes Christopher Fulford, Patrick Malahide, Mary Jo Randle, David Ryall

Jeremy Boynton in Driven to Distraction *is an undoubted bounder. But is he a killer too?*

DRUGS

Half-way through the plot of *The Settling of the Sun* – a murder committed among foreign-language students – traces of heroin are found in the students' bus. The drug's spectral entrance on the scene changes everything for Morse. He is never so happy as when he is plotting the violent interactions brought about by lust, jealousy, ambition and disappointment. But drugs are a random element, unpredictable and intractable. Any evidence of their involvement in a case makes him miserable – and not just because the obnoxious DEWAR will inevitably be launched at him.

'I can't handle drugs,' Morse says despondently. 'I can't work out why they do it. Beyond me.' Lewis's laconic answer to this is as pragmatic as ever. 'Same reason you drink beer.' But predictably Morse will have none of this. 'Beer is food,' he replies acidly.

The *Morse* film that has the most to do with drugs is *Cherubim and Seraphim*, a sombre story which examines the accelerated trajectory of the drug-taker – the excitement of their surge to the peak of happiness and then the plunge into darkness that immediately follows. When Marilyn Garrett kills herself it is because, as Morse grimly describes it, she believes she has experienced total happiness through the drug:

> 'That's what's *really* wicked. To make you think you've seen everything there is to see at sixteen. That you've had the best of life before it's even begun. To make you think there's nothing left to live for. I hope that man's in hellfire now.'

In this film, too, Lewis reveals that he once smoked cannabis, though it just 'made my head spin'. We could never imagine Morse as a user – but in one sense he does 'use' drugs. In *Last Seen Wearing* he blackmails the young man Maguire with his knowledge that he uses cannabis, forcing him to reveal what he knows about the missing Valerie. In the later film version, Maguire's drug of choice is cocaine. In both cases, Morse is contemptuous of the man.

· E ·

EAGLE AND CHILD

Standing on St Giles', and otherwise known as 'The Bird and Baby', this PUBLIC HOUSE was the favourite meeting place in the 1940s and 1950s of the so-called 'Inklings' – the informal beer-drinking club which included C. S. Lewis and J. R. R. Tolkien among its members. The back bar of the pub has a plaque celebrating the connection with these renowned writers, but in *The Secret of Annexe 3*: 13, when Morse and Lewis spend an evening there poring over the details of the case before them, Lewis fantasizes about another plaque up on the wall: 'CHIEF INSPECTOR MORSE, with his friend and colleague Sergeant Lewis, sat in this back room one Thursday, in order to solve . . .'

The Eagle and Child, a pub with famous literary associations.

EDUCATION

Investigating the ROGER BACON COMPREHENSIVE SCHOOL in *Last Seen Wearing*: 7 Morse casts a sceptical eye over Valerie Taylor's curriculum:

> 'Environmental Studies', he doubted, was little more than a euphemism for occasional visits to the gasworks, the fire station and the sewage installations; whilst for Sociology and sociologists he had nothing but sour contempt . . . With such a plethora of non-subjects crowding the timetable there was no room for the traditional disciplines taught in his own day.

Morse, like his creator, consistently deplores the turn modern education has taken.

Yet in *Cherubim and Seraphim*, he finds himself facing the fact that the modern world requires fresh educational attitudes. Looking in on a sex-education ('Personal and Social Development') class, he is disconcerted to see the blown-up condoms being bounced around by the pupils but is forced to admit that this new openness is a good thing. Later, during the same visit, he is berated by Greenhill, a passionate young English teacher who taught his niece Marilyn. Tentatively Morse had suggested that Marilyn's suicide may have had something to do with Sylvia Plath's presence on the syllabus. Greenhill replies angrily, 'I utterly reject your implication . . . Sylvia Plath committed suicide and teenagers are so sensitive it's not safe to let them read her poems? . . . You know, if you policemen had your way, no one would ever be taught to read or write . . . One hears that point of view so often these days and it's so *crass*.'

As it turns out, Greenhill is quite right. The enormous irony of this episode is that Marilyn's suicide is because of a chemical experience of perfect happiness. It has nothing whatever to do with her educational analysis of Plath's, or anyone else's, suicidal misery.

ENGLISH LANGUAGE, THE

Morse is a linguistic conservative and makes no apology for it. Indeed, he is consistently preoccupied with the grammatical usage and the spelling of those around him – a lone voice in the KIDLINGTON police station crying out against 'due to' instead of 'owing to', Ms instead of Miss, 'would of' instead of 'would have'.

It is usually Lewis who receives the dubious benefit of Morse's pedantry as he does in the film of *Death is Now My Neighbour*:

LEWIS: Death would have been instant, would it, doctor?
MORSE: Occurred *instantaneously*, Lewis. Or 'was instantaneous', if you must. Coffee may be instant, death may not.

And again, in *Last Bus to Woodstock*: 4, 'That was the most ill-written report I've seen in years with twelve – no less – grammatical monstrosities in ten lines! What's the force coming to?'

Morse attempts to maintain high standards himself. His vocabulary is extensive – 'He does crosswords, madam,' Lewis tells Lady Hanbury in *The Ghost in the Machine*. 'He knows all sorts of words that nobody ever uses.' Unusual words that either Dexter or Morse use and enjoy include dolichocephalic (*The Secret of Annexe 3*: 11), kyphotic ('Dead as a Dodo'), steatopygous (*The Inside Story*), melismatic and boustrophedon (*Service of All the Dead*: 10 and 34).

Morse's working knowledge of *Fowler's Modern English Usage* cannot be said to be of daily utility, but it does occasionally come in handy. In *The Ghost in the Machine* he is sure Sir Julius's 'suicide' note is fake because it has 'apologise' rather than the more etymologically correct 'apologize'. Correct grammar also has more personal uses. In *The*

Daughters of Cain: 68, Morse receives a declaration of love from Ellie Smith, the young prostitute, and is momentarily covered in confusion. He hides his emotions from Lewis with the following Mr Chips-like remark: 'If I ever see her again, Lewis, I shall have to tell her that "rang" is the more correct form of the past tense of the verb "to ring", when used transitively.'

EPIGRAPH(S)

Except in *Service of All the Dead* and *The Silent World of Nicholas Quinn*, Dexter never fails to grace each chapter he writes with an epigraph and, since he specializes in exceptionally short chapters, he needs a great many pithy and apposite quotations. They range over a wide spectrum of learning, from the classical poets to Mills and Boon. But the reader of Morse novels should take care before requoting these tags, especially when the author is not known or not named. Is there such a book as Donet's *Elementary Latin Syntax*? Are such eminent personages as Diogenes SMALL (later Viscount Mumbles) real? Who was the poet Lilian Cooper who apparently supplied the title and epigraph for *The Jewel That Was Ours*? Is '*Initium est dimidium facti*' (Once you've started, you're half-way there) a genuine Latin proverb?

It is not surprising, since the author and his hero are classicists, that the Greeks and Romans are frequently cited. Philip Larkin and T. S. Eliot crop up more than any other modern poets, and Shaw's 'I enjoy convalescence; it is the part that makes the illness worth while', from the play *Back to Methuselah*, is used in two separate books, *The Wench is Dead*: 37 and *The Daughters of Cain*: 6.

There is a variation on the epigraph technique in *The Riddle of the Third Mile*, where at the head of each chapter Dexter, in eighteenth-century style, has an enticingly 'In which . . .' summary of events which follow. Chapter 19, for example, is headed 'Our two detectives have not yet quite finished with the implications of severe dismemberment'.

· F ·

FAMILIES

Damaged families – the violence and pain underlying a household whose relations are riven by jealousy and betrayal – are a major preoccupation of Morse on film. Such situations form the basis for the dramas – and the murders – in *Greeks Bearing Gifts, The Ghost in the Machine, Happy Families, The Infernal Serpent, The Sins of the Fathers* and *The Settling of the Sun*, though the theme enters in one way or another into the majority of episodes. Oddly, however, there is no comparable vein in Dexter's novels, which tend to be more concerned with the childless and with dramas about professional relationships in the workplace.

Morse, himself is, of course, childless and knows hardly anything about modern family life. Lewis is therefore an invaluable guide to him, leading him where necessary through the murky underworld of babies, bath times, birthdays, school sportsdays, wives' knitting bees and the like. Lewis struggles bravely to resist Morse's bachelor contempt for normal working hours, but when Morse tells him, after yet another extended shift, to 'go home and kiss his children', Lewis knows that his wife, Valerie, at her wits' end, is more likely to have arranged for him to give them a good hiding. 'I'm more like the executioner in our house than the father,' he complains. Such is the policeman's lot, if he is also a family man.

The Copley-Barnes family has poison at its heart in The Infernal Serpent.

FAT CHANCE (TV film only)

FEMINISM is an undercurrent – or more accurately a counter-current – in Morse's world, where he scarcely tries to conceal his ingrained male chauvinism. But of all the episodes, this one presents his most head-on collison with feminist ideals. A society of Christian women running a women's refuge are campaigning for women priests in the Church of England – and in particular for one of them to be the new chaplain at ST SAVIOUR'S COLLEGE. A most un-Christian attitude towards the women is adopted by their traditionalist High Church opponents. But did they murder Dr Victoria Hazlett, who wanted to be a priest? And are they trying to murder another member of the collective, a leading candidate for the college chaplaincy?

Fat Chance: *made when an image like this still had the power to shock.*

Morse's view is typically caustic: 'I reckon we're seeing a particularly Oxford view of things, Lewis. Extreme images. God as a prissy old don nit-picking his way through the Liturgy versus God as a muscular Girl Guide.' But no sooner are the words out of his mouth than he meets the organizer of this particular women's group, Emma Pickford (Zoë Wanamaker). 'Dib, dib, dib, sir!' remarks Lewis, when he sees the Chief Inspector's face go strangely slack, and Morse seems to spend the rest of the episode looking for excuses to be in Emma's company.

The other strand in this complex film concerns that most feminist of issues – fat. Freddie Galt (Kenneth Haigh) is the latest of several cynical gurus in the world of Morse, making money out of the gullibility of vulnerable people. He has grown rich running the Think Thin health farm, a pseudo-evangelical organization which actually bases its (suspiciously short-term) results on a dubious drug. But Galt has a dissatisfied client, the obese Dinah Newberry (played with great panache by Caroline Ryder), who is on the rampage in revenge against the health farm for what she sees as its poisonous slimming drug. When it turns out that she is not far wrong, and that this slimmer's nostrum can be fatal in combination with other everyday substances, the key to the case is turned.

In many cases, only Morse can see an 'incidental' death for the murder that it really is. But here the reverse is true: the apparent 'murder' turns out to be something not less sinister but unexpectedly different.

First transmission 27 February 1991
Writer Alma Cullen
Director Roy Battersby
Cast includes Maurice Denham, Kenneth Haigh, Peggy Mount, Maggie O'Neill, Caroline Ryder, Zoë Wanamaker

FEMINISM

CLAIRE: Tide of global feminism passed you by, then?

MORSE: In that respect I'm with Canute all the way. (*The Way Through the Woods*)

Morse is many times confronted with his own unrepentant male chauvinism. One notable occasion is an exchange with a woman police officer, Nora Curtis, in *The Day of the Devil*, where Morse is foolish enough to mention that women on motorbikes do not exactly accord with his notion of the finest feminine qualities: 'I can sum up your idea of feminine qualities in one word – weakness. And it's that weakness that sustains discrimination, inequality and violence in all its forms. From the statutory slap in the mouth to the kind of thing we get from the bastard we're all chasing.' Morse retreats to lick his wounds after this bruising encounter.

'A monstrous regiment of women'. Morse finds himself investigating a feminist collective in Fat Chance.

Emma Pickford can make feminism seem attractive even to Morse in Fat Chance.

Another sharp reminder that his attitudes about gender are twenty years out of date comes when he casually addresses Dr Laura HOBSON as 'my dear'. She replies:

> I am not your 'dear'. You must forgive me for being blunt: but I am no one's 'luv' or 'dear' or 'darling' or 'sweetheart'. I've got a name. If I'm at work I prefer to be called Dr Hobson; and if I let my hair down over a drink, I have a Christian name: Laura. That's my little speech, Chief Inspector. You're not the first to have heard it.

Morse seems rather less chastened by this excoriation than he should be and is soon musing on the doctor's attractive north-country vowels and 'the not unpleasant prospect of meeting her sometime over a drink with her hair down'.

Fat Chance and *Driven to Distraction* are the two films which most thoroughly chew over feminist issues. Working in *Driven to Distraction* with Detective Sergeant Siobhan Maitland, an expert on crimes against women, Morse is typically recalcitrant and provocative. But by the end, the two officers have developed a mutual respect, each seeing in the other their own intelligence and stubbornness, however differently expressed, reflected back. In *Fat Chance*, a film about women priests and a fraudulent health farm, Morse's normally combative sexism is a beast perhaps rather too easily tamed by the charms of Emma Pickford (Zoë Wanamaker).

FIGHTS

Morse's favourite weapon is his mind and he rarely gets into physical fights. The struggle with Harry Josephs, however, at the climax of *Service of All the Dead*: 35 – mainly because it is a fight over a woman – does succeed in bringing out in him all 'the strangely compelling and primitive instinct of the hunter for the hunted'. This instinct nearly costs him his life, for in actual combat he proves no match for the jungle training and fitness of his adversary. At another highly charged moment, the climax of the TV version of *The Way Through the Woods*, he tries to draw the gunfire away from Lewis and towards himself, and when that fails, he attacks with a shovel, felling the shotgun-wielding aggressor with a single blow.

Morse's verbal aggression more often takes the form of sarcasm, but there can be a surprisingly direct and rude side to his behaviour, as when, in *Last Seen Wearing*: 8, he forces his way into a strip club (though it helps of course that he has Lewis with him):

> 'Look, you miserable sod. You want a fight? That's fine. I wouldn't want to bruise my fist against your ugly chops myself, but this pal of mine will do it with the greatest of pleasure. Just up his street. Army middleweight champion till a year ago. Where shall we go, you dirty little squit?'

As befits a man morally anchored in the 1950s, there is more than a hint of Dick Barton, Special Agent, about his tone of voice here.

'Shoot me!' Morse dices with death in The Way Through the Woods.

FLAT, MORSE'S

We learn in *The Way Through the Woods*: 21 that Morse's bachelor flat is in Leys Close, North Oxford, between the Banbury Road and the Woodstock Road. It is sparsely but tastefully furnished in old-fashioned style, with 'the heavy old walnut suite his mother had left him' (*The Riddle of the Third Mile*: 27) and 'the family heirloom – nest of tables – Chippendale, 1756' ('Neighbourhood Watch') as the most important items of furniture. Few other details are given in the novels, but from what can be seen in the films, its walls are hung with good prints and there is a prominent armillary sphere on the table (*The Settling of the Sun*).

When, in *Dead on Time*, Susan Fallon, Morse's old love, comes to the flat, she feels it betokens something about him:

> MORSE: I can't *imagine* what this place has to say about me.
> SUSAN: Oh, a sturdy self-sufficiency, a certain contentment.

Although it is doubtful Morse would himself see it like that, his home is undoubtedly a retreat, an important oasis of solitary, musical, whiskied calm. This is why, when the gutter journalists in *Happy Families* invade his privacy there, his outrage is fuelled by the sense of personal violation.

In filming, the location used for Morse's flat is nowhere near Oxford but is, in fact, in Ealing, a part of west London developed at exactly the same time and in the same style as North Oxford.

Morse's flat fire-bombed by Hugo de Vries in Masonic Mysteries. *His entire record collection is melted.*

FOOD

Morse has very little interest in food. He had a microwave oven once, he tells Anthony Donn in *Deceived by Flight*, 'but we fought'. Most of Morse's calories come in the form of beer – a fact with worrying consequences for his HEALTH.

FOREIGN EXAMINATIONS SYNDICATE

The setting for the events described in *The Silent World of Nicholas Quinn* is a large house in CHAUCER ROAD. Although loosely based on the Oxford Delegacy of Local Examinations, the Syndicate is far smaller, deals with overseas schools using the British public examinations system and is governed by a board of twelve Syndics, 'each a prominent fellow of his or her college within the University of Oxford'. These worthies are seen in the first chapter of the novel deliberating over the appointment of a new graduate member of staff, who, after considerable dissension, will be the profoundly deaf but ideally qualified eponymous Quinn.

FREEMASONRY

In the film *Masonic Mysteries*, Morse is a member of the chorus singing in an amateur production of Mozart's *The Magic Flute*. The opera is a masonic work, as Morse's adversary Chief Inspector Bottomley, an enthusiastic member of the local masonic lodge, points out.

Modern Freemasonry is an eighteenth-century invention, a network of idealistic social clubs using rituals adapted from what were then regarded as the traditions of the medieval craft guilds. Mozart was particularly attracted to a Viennese lodge associated with progressive rationalism and joined it in 1784. He went on to write more than a dozen works in which, by means of musical tonality and rhythm, he makes coded references to the 'craft'. *The Magic Flute* is his most famous and comprehensive exercise in the genre.

'There's always one!' Morse has forgotten his medallion in Masonic Mysteries.

Freemasonry is today rather less associated in the public mind with enlightened rationality. If it were, Morse would at least consider membership of Bottomley's lodge, even though as he says, 'I don't join things.' In fact, Morse is uncomfortable with all forms of 'flummery', whether it be masonic or ritual, university ceremonial or the traditions of the aristocracy. This is an important source of friction between himself and Bottomley, leading indirectly to Morse's arrest for the murder of Beryl Newsome.

This film was a topical item when it was first screened, for masonry in the police force was being much discussed in Britain in the early 1990s. In *Deadly Slumber* it is referred to again when Lewis teases STRANGE about his membership of the lodge.

· G ·

GAMBLING

> 'It's this whole business of *chance*, Lewis. We don't go in much for talking about chance and luck, and what a huge part they play in our lives. But the Greeks did – *and* the Romans; they both used to worship the goddess of luck. *The Riddle of the Third Mile*: 19.

Morse has a compulsive personality and sheds his habits with uncommon difficulty. However, he does seem to be something of a reformed gambler, according to *The Jewel That Was Ours*: 37, when he admits to having lost a lot of money in the past. Now he regards betting on the turf, not very originally, as 'a mug's game . . . A dirty game too'.

Dexter's thoughts on gambling are roughly similar. A short disquisition, almost a homily, on 'the urge to gamble, so universal, so deeply embedded in unregenerate human nature' appears in *Last Seen Wearing*: 21, and here the psychological and cultural aspects of betting and the appalling destructiveness of its cruel inequalities are set out.

In that novel bingo is cast as Mother's Ruin, for Valerie Taylor's mother is a compulsive bingo player. In *Service of All the Dead*, betting on horses is Harry Joseph's ruinous vice. Yet in *Deadly Slumber*, the gambling of the bookmaker Michael Steppings has been an easy route to wealth:

MORSE: You make it sound easy – making money.
STEPPINGS: It was – how I made it. Gambling. I liked it. I was good at it.
MORSE: I don't think I could live with the uncertainty.

If Morse is indeed a gambler who saw the light, we would expect occasional backsliding. The perfect example of this comes in *Last Bus to Woodstock*: 3, when Morse – together with a reluctant Lewis, under quite unfair pressure from his Chief Inspector – backs a horse. Lewis intends an each-way bet and is mocked for his timidity, but when the horse comes in second, it is Morse who hedged the bet and made the profit.

GHOST IN THE MACHINE, THE (TV film only)

Competition for academic preferment would again seem to be the mainspring of the plot here, with intense rivalry for the Mastership of COURTENAY COLLEGE between Sir Julius Hanbury, an aristocrat, ex-diplomat and man of the world, and Professor Ullman, 'one of the most distinguished scholars the university can boast'. But as soon as some of Sir

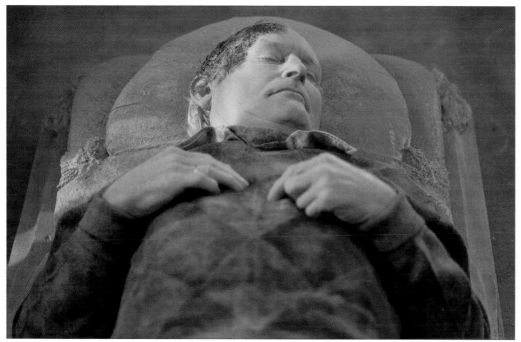

Sir Julius Hanbury, as he is found in The Ghost in the Machine, *laid out on a tomb in the family chapel.*

Julius's favourite lubricious paintings of slave girls by Alma-Tadema are (apparently) stolen and the baronet himself is discovered laid out in his private chapel with massive head wounds, the centre of attention moves to HANBURY HALL and the Hanbury family. And the more Morse pokes around, armed with some puzzling information about the wounds from the new female PATHOLOGIST, Dr Russell

RUSSELL: Well, I realize I'm not Max.
MORSE: Thank God for that, he never tells me anything.

the less interested he is in Professor Ullman. Now it is the busty French nanny whom Lady Hanbury has suddenly sacked, the over-protective old retainer 'Maltby', the handsome Harrovian odd-job man and the secret photographic studio in the attic that engage his interest. Then the outline of an entirely different plot begins to form in his brain: 'God, how the rich do carry on. An impotent husband and a pretty *au pair*, a doting gardener and a jealous chatelaine . . . You live in a place like this, you think the rules don't apply. Delusions of grandeur.'

First transmission 25 March 1992
Writer Adrian Mitchell, based on an idea by Colin Dexter
Director Herbert Wise
Cast includes Patsy Byrne, Patricia Hodge, Bernard Lloyd

GILL'S THE IRONMONGERS

Gill & Co., 128a High Street, are an Oxford institution, reputed to be the country's (which probably means the world's) oldest ironmonger's shop, dating back to 1530. The stock is enormous, some of it reputed to go back if not to the sixteenth century then to before metrication – a quality that would surely appeal strongly to Morse. It is the shop in the film version of *Last Bus to Woodstock* where young Sanders works before he is summarily sacked for bad timekeeping.

GREEKS BEARING GIFTS (TV film only)

Nicos, the chef of Lewis's favourite Greek restaurant, is murdered and Morse has a bad-tempered exchange with the restaurant's owner, Greek shipping millionaire Basilios Vasilakis. To the consternation of STRANGE (after consulting *Who's Who*), Vasilakis is a member of the Athenaeum, has an OBE and has 'married into our nobility, a generous benefactor and chairman of God knows how many charities'. Morse, however, is flatly unimpressed by these links with the British Establishment: 'Ethnic cases aren't up my street. Don't speak the language. Don't receive the signals people of the same race make to each other, or else try to conceal . . .'

At first Morse seems justified in seeing this as a matter internal to the local Greek community. The murder of the chef is to do with his sister Maria's illegitimate baby, conceived and born in Greece but brought to Oxford when she travels to attend Nicos's funeral. But when she too is murdered and the baby is kidnapped, Morse is forced to widen his inquiries to include Randall Rees (Martin Jarvis), a classics don at an unnamed Oxford college, his wife, Friday, a TV agony aunt, the theme-park entrepreneur Digby Tuckerman (James Hazeldine) and a replica of a Greek trireme, the warship that saved Greek civilization.

Nichols's script makes much of the contrast between the respect people have for ancient Greek culture and their subliminal racism towards modern Greeks – 'bubbles' from 'a Third World country on the fringes of Europe', as Vasilakis puts it. Morse feels himself above such ignorant prejudices – 'That's not a view that an educated man would take' – but Vasilakis sharply corrects him:

> VASILAKIS: An educated man, in England for example, always makes a clear distinction between the glory that was Greece and the mess it is today. There were the Athenians and now there are the savages who replaced them, who aren't even capable of looking after their own antiquities.
>
> MORSE: I thought it wouldn't be long before we got round to the Elgin Marbles.

Echoes of ancient Greece resound through this script. Morse reminds Digby Tuckerman at one point not to fly, like Icarus, too close to the sun, and later there is an argument at the Oxford Union about whether war could be justified in defence of the Athenian

Faced with his distraught wife at the top of the stairs, Randall Rees tries to reason with her, as Morse looks on – and finally learns the truth – in a scene from Greeks Bearing Gifts.

democracy. Then, in the last words of the film, Morse tells Lewis of Virgil's line from Book II of *The Aeneid*: *'Timeo Danaos et dona ferentes'* (I fear the Greeks, even when they bear gifts).

First transmission 20 March 1991
Writer Peter Nichols
Director Adrian Shergold
Cast includes James Faulkner, Jan Harvey, James Hazeldine, Martin Jarvis, Richard Pearson.

· H ·

HANBURY HALL

The seat of Sir Julius Hanbury, *The Ghost in the Machine*, with its 'important gardens', is in fact Stowe Landscape Gardens in Buckinghamshire.

HAPPY FAMILIES (TV film only)

Curzon Engineering is 'one of the top twenty companies in the country', as Lewis tells Morse. It had been inherited by Lady Emily Balcombe from her father and was now run

Daggers drawn: Harry Balcombe meets his end in Happy Families.

by her husband, Sir John, and two unmarried sons, Harry and James. This is 'serious money', but all is not well in the Balcombe family, living in their gloomy, draughty, moated castle. The 'boys' are treated like recalcitrant children by their father, and behave accordingly. Lady Emily is strangely detached and distant.

Morse and Lewis are called to the castle when Sir John, a boorish and charmless individual, is found murdered. Never at ease with the aristocracy, Morse's discomfort is exacerbated when he finds himself bracketed with this same leisured class by a cynical tabloid journalist. This renegade and embittered Oxford man picks Morse as the unique angle for his story, building a series of articles round what he sees as Morse's laziness and cultural superiority.

Finding his own personality and tastes held up to public scrutiny infuriates the reticent Morse, but he is forced to put it in perspective when James, just before his own death, reminds him, 'Well, look on the bright side. You could be me. My father and brother have been murdered – that's *real* persecution.'

The opening sequence of the film, in which Lady Emily's birthday party is climaxed with her husband's murder, is a small masterpiece of Gothic tragicomedy. From the first flushing toilet to the mad gleam in Lady Emily's eyes when Sir John's body is found, Shergold's direction is clever and atmospheric, surrounding the characters with darkness and shadows and adding a gleeful, doom-laden rhythm to the editing.

The Balcombe castle scenes were shot at a private castle in Oxfordshire.

First transmission 11 March 1992
Writer Daniel Boyle
Director Adrian Shergold
Cast includes Alun Armstrong, Martin Clunes, Charlotte Coleman, Jonathan Coy, Rupert Graves, Anna Massey, Andrew Ray, Gwen Taylor

HARDEN, ROY

The concierge at the RANDOLPH HOTEL, who retired after exactly fifty years' service, having started at the hotel as a boy of fourteen. Colin Dexter spoke at his farewell party. He is mentioned in *The Jewel That Was Ours* and is seen in the film *The Wolvercote Tongue*.

HEADINGTON

At the heart of this area of north-east Oxford is the modern JOHN RADCLIFFE HOSPITAL, which is connected to the High and St Clement Street by the Headington Road. On the left of this road as you travel up towards the hospital is Headington Hill Hall. This imposing Victorian mansion was the home of the disgraced press baron Robert Maxwell and it was from here Maxwell used to run the Pergamon Press, publisher of Colin Dexter's co-authored textbooks in the 1960s. While Maxwell lived there, the house was

Headington Hill Hall, c. 1900.

owned by Oxford City Council, making him the most luxuriously housed council tenant in the country (see TWILIGHT OF THE GODS).

Manor Road, home ground of Oxford United Football Club, where Morse and Lewis watch half of a rainy game in *Service of All the Dead*: 15, is in Headington.

HEALTH

Morse has a low tolerance for pain. In *The Riddle of the Third Mile* and *The Last Enemy* we find him suffering from severe toothache and he is such a coward in the face of the chair and the drill that he receives a severe lecture from his dentist: 'For heaven's sake, be a man, Inspector. If this is the way you behave when facing some slight discomfort, no wonder violent crime is on the increase.'

Apart from this aberration – and an accident in *Last Bus to Woodstock* when he falls off a ladder and injures his foot – Morse's physical health is rarely an issue in the early novels and films. But from *The Wench is Dead* onwards, his smoking, lack of exercise and refusal to take an adequate proportion of his calories in solid form begin to take a heavy toll on his constitution. Morse lands up in hospital with serious illness in three out of the last five novels, and readers have thereby become thoroughly familar with the Chief Inspector's claret and blue pyjamas, 'as gaudily striped as a Lido deckchair'.

In *The Wench is Dead*, it is a perforated ulcer that consigns Morse to the JOHN RAD-CLIFFE HOSPITAL's Ward 7C. In *The Daughters of Cain*, he is back again, his diseases now multiplying. As he explains to his bedside visitor, Chief Superintendent STRANGE:

'I'm suffering from bronchi-something beginning with "e"; my liver and kidneys are disintegrating; my blood pressure isn't quite off the top of the scale – not yet; I'm nursing another stomach ulcer; and as if that wasn't enough I'm on the verge of diabetes . . . oh yes, and my cholesterol's dangerously high.' (34)

And in the next novel, *Death is Now My Neighbour*, Morse's incipient diabetes is diagnosed and, chronically tired and with a persistent headache, he returns home:

to take four daily readings of his blood-sugar level using a slim penlike instrument into which he inserted a test-strip duly smeared with a drop of his blood . . . Now thus far readings had been roughly what Morse had been led to expect: it would take some little while – and then only if he promised to do what he was told – to achieve that 'balance' which is the aim of every diabetic. (50)

The search for balance, though, is a worthy undertaking for a disciple of ARISTOTLE like Morse, so he settles down to add yet another name to the list of things he is dependent on: insulin.

HEROES, MORSE'S

Morse has a trio of principal heroes, ARISTOTLE, A. E. HOUSMAN AND WAGNER. In terms of other detectives, he occasionally cites the incomparable Sherlock Holmes as an influence, and certainly there is much of Holmes in his make-up. Both men insist on cerebration as a means of solving crimes, both resort to psychoactive substances (though Morse takes not a 7 per cent solution of cocaine but a pint or three of cask-conditioned beer) and both are bachelors – though in Morse's case not without occasional regrets. However, the big difference between Morse and Holmes is in 'method'. Holmes is big on deduction, backed up by keen observation, research and record-keeping. Morse has the police computer whenever he wants it, but his method of making random connections to see where they lead – 'blundering about', he calls it – would be anathema to Holmes.

Within the police force there is only one figure who could be described as a hero of Morse: his old Chief Inspector, Desmond MCNUTT.

Sherlock Holmes, as played in 1907 by William Gillette.

HOBSON, DR LAURA

The PATHOLOGIST who takes over in the Morse novels when Max dies is a good-looking woman 'in her early thirties, fair-complexioned, with a pair of disproportionately large spectacles on her pretty nose; a smallish woman, about 5 foot 4 inches'.

Needless to say, in spite of the stern lecture on FEMINISM she gives him after he calls her 'my dear', Morse is soon noticing 'the slim curve of her legs' and fantasizing about squiring her around Oxford. It is beginning to look like Dr Grayling RUSSELL all over again.

Dr Hobson is the pathologist in the novels *The Way Through the Woods*, *The Daughters of Cain* and *Death is Now My Neighbour*. She is also in the equivalent television films, played by Clare Holman.

Dr Hobson gets down to another body in The Daughters of Cain.

HOLIDAY(S)

Morse does not much like holidays though he feels he ought to take them occasionally. 'Mostly I haven't been quite so miserable since last year's holiday,' he writes glumly in a postcard to Lewis from Lyme Regis in *The Way Through the Woods*: 16.

Service of All the Dead: 6 lays out Morse's general lackadaisical approach to the question of his annual leave. In January he starts to fantasize: 'He had never been to Greece and . . . retained enough romance in his soul to imagine a lazy liaison with some fading film star beside the wine-dark waves of the Aegean.' But 'dilatoriness and indecisiveness' ensure that 'instead, on this chilly Monday mid-morning in early April, he stood at a bus-stop in North Oxford, with a fortnight's furlough before him, wondering exactly how other people could organize their lives, make decisions, write a letter even'.

However, on other occasions, he goes to Italy to indulge in 'cultural pursuits', and he also gets sufficiently organized to travel to southern Germany for the annual *Wagnerfest* on at least one occasion (in the film version of *The Way Through the Woods*):

STRANGE: You've no idea what it was like here last summer . . . You only caught the tail end of it. You were off sunning yourself in Beirut.
MORSE: Bayreuth, sir.

As the short story 'Morse's Greatest Mystery' shows, Morse is even less enthusiastic about Christmas. He uses the enforced lay-off to stay crabbily by himself, re-reading Dickens, redecorating the flat – anything but celebrate in the traditional way. But, on the occasion described in the story, something he cannot account for enters his soul and he makes a large and unconventionally managed charitable donation. He finds a holiday pleasure in this act: a holiday from his accustomed stinginess with MONEY.

HOUSMAN, ALFRED EDWARD

Housman (1859–1936), professor of Latin at University College, London, and then Cambridge, is one of Morse's favourite writers. The life of this scholar-poet, whose most famous work is *A Shropshire Lad*, finds parallel at several points in that of the policeman. Both men went up to St John's College, Oxford, to read Greats. Both formed a passionate attachment at university (though in Housman's case, since he was homosexual, it was with a man, Moses Jackson) and were left by their lovers. Both then failed their finals and spent the rest

of their lives in a state of heightened, even luxuriant despondency. Housman also had a liking for mild PORNOGRA-PHY, to judge by his publication in 1931 (in Germany) of *Praefenda*, a mock-scholarly anthology of bawdiness and obscenity from Latin authors.

Lines from Housman turn up as chapter EPIGRAPHS in a number of Morse novels: *The Dead of Jericho*: 4 and 16, *Last Seen Wearing*: 40, *The Daughters of Cain*: 9 and 15, *Death is Now My Neighbour*: 44 and *The Way Through the Woods*: 47. In the short story 'The Inside Story', Housman becomes part of a clue when Morse discovers in the room of the dead Sheila Poster (who owns Housman's *Collected Poems*) a postcard addressed to her and inscribed only with lines from a Housman love poem:

And wide apart we lie, my love,
And seas between the twain.

Scholar–poet A. E. Housman, photographed c. *1910.*

· I ·

INFERNAL SERPENT, THE (TV film only)

Immediately prior to delivering a controversial speech, Dr Julian Dear, the saintly and eminent environmentalist of BEAUFORT COLLEGE, is mugged, suffers a heart attack and dies. The college's Master, Copley-Barnes, has investments in a chemical company whose misdeeds Dear was about to expose. Is this the reason for Dear's death?

But there are worse things happening. Someone is posting disgusting parcels to the Master's Lodge: a bucket of rotting fish, a sheep's head, the skin of a snake. Meanwhile, the investigative journalist Sylvie Maxton, long known to the Copley-Barneses, has

Geoffrey Palmer is menacingly evil as the Master of Lonsdale in The Infernal Serpent.

arrived in Oxford to write a profile of the Master. As a child, she was unofficially adopted by the family and she knows more than anybody about the Master's deeper secrets – the serpent 'coiled around the foundations' of a house whose evil lives on and will replicate itself until it can be stopped. There is more than one character who would like to bring about this end: the college gardener, whose daughter has been abused; Sylvie herself, with her memories of holidays at the beach; and perhaps even the Master's apparently devoted wife.

Cullen's screenplay and Madden's direction lend a fine, doom-laden quality to this film. The story is a classical tragedy in essence: the house of a powerful man infected with past evil, while those around him are possessed by fear and the certainty of retribution, though they cannot tell in what guise it will come. Putting in a performance utterly different from his many TV sitcoms, Geoffrey Palmer invests the role of the Master with a looming nastiness that is truly unsettling.

First transmission 3 January 1990
Writer Alma Cullen
Director John Madden
Cast includes Cheryl Campbell, Barbara Leigh-Hunt, Geoffrey Palmer, Tom Wilkinson

'INSIDE STORY, THE' (short story, 1993)

The sage teenager Diogenes SMALL comes to the assistance of Morse when his book *Reflections on Inspiration and Creativity* is found beside the bedside of a murder victim. One particular sentence is highlighted, stressing that the creative writer must mix reality and experience with carefully chosen 'fictional addenda' to 'elevate our earth-bound artist . . . on the wings of creativity and freedom'. The clue means little enough at first, but when Morse discovers that the late Ms Sheila Poster (under the anagrammatical pseudonym Elissa Thorpe) has entered a detective-story competition, he realizes that the story must contain clues as to why someone felt it necessary to plunge a knife into her heart. Applying to Rex de Lincto, the Oxford Book Association's chairman and organizer of the competition, he reads her story avidly. If he can just disentangle fact from fiction, he will be able to identify the murderer.

INSPECTOR MORSE SOCIETY, THE

The Society was founded by a group of Sherlock Holmes enthusiasts in 1997. Meetings and weekends are arranged for members and there is a newsletter, 'Endeavour'. Address: c/o Antony Richards, 170 Woodland Road, Sawston, Cambridge CB2 4DX. Website: http://mesmsg1.me.ic.ac.uk/sherlock

ITALY

See DEATH OF THE SELF, THE.

· J ·

JAGUAR

See CAR.

JERICHO

The setting for much of the novel and film *The Dead of Jericho* was originally a poor, working-class ghetto between the RADCLIFFE INFIRMARY and the Oxford CANAL. Jericho's first inhabitants were workers from the nearby Oxford University Press, railwaymen and craftspeople. Its parish church, St Barnabas ('Barnie's') in Cardigan Street, was built by the Pre-Raphaelite patron Thomas Combe, whose instructions to his architect, Arthur Blomfield, were that 'not a penny was to be thrown away on external appearance and decoration'.

Canal Reach, in which the novel's Anne Scott lives and dies, is fictional but in the film Coombe Road substitutes. This first *Morse* film, unlike most of the others, was shot entirely in Oxford.

Jericho features largely in the fictional universe of another English novelist – and one of Morse's favourites – Thomas Hardy. It is here, renamed as Beersheba, in the parish of 'St Silas', that Jude Fawley in *Jude the Obscure* comes to live while he makes his disastrous attempt to break into the academic life of Christminster. It is here too that the tragedy of his children's deaths occurs– 'done because we are too menny' (sic).

Jericho in 1851, with the Oxford University Press on the right.

JEWEL THAT WAS OURS, THE (novel, 1991)

> Downes sometimes felt a bit dubious about 'Americans'; yet, like almost all his colleagues
> in Oxford, he found himself enjoying actual Americans. (*The Jewel That Was Ours*: 17)

Cedric Downes is one of three learned academics – the others being Theodore Kemp of the ASHMOLEAN MUSEUM and the hard-drinking Sheila Williams – who have been engaged to impart wisdom to a group of upmarket and elderly American cultural tourists arriving in 'Arksford'. One of the ladies is carrying with her the 'Wolvercote Tongue', part of a jewelled Anglo-Saxon belt which had been bought by her late first husband and which she now intends to present to Dr Kemp for the museum, where the rest of the buckle resides. But before she so much as kicks off her shoes in the suite at the RANDOLPH HOTEL, she has keeled over with a fatal coronary. By the time she is found, the Tongue has gone.

The group of squabbling, discontented, contrary, mischievous, near-geriatric Americans form a lively background to Morse's investigation, first into the disappearing Tongue and then the subsequent untimely demise of Dr Kemp, 'one of the most dedicated womanizers in the university'. For below the suave, well-educated surface of the three Oxford lives thrashes the same maelstrom of avarice, gluttony, sloth, lust, envy, pride and anger that are the fundamentals of all Dexter novels. Everyone is concealing something, so that, as Morse himself points out, 'One of the secrets of solving murders is never to believe anybody – not completely – not at the start.'

But, as ever, Morse does not apply the art of scepticism with as much dedication to his own theories as he does to the statements of others and many a beautiful but erroneous hypothesis is built up, as precarious as a pagoda made of playing cards, before the full devious and complex truth is revealed to him.

The EPIGRAPH to this book also provided the novel's title: a quatrain with the name Lilian Cooper (1904–81) attached:

> Espied the god with gloomy soul
> The prize that in the casket lay
> Who came with silent tread and stole
> The jewel that was ours away.

Interested readers may search for more luminous lines by this obviously gifted poet but they will do so in vain. The name is borrowed from Colin Dexter's own mother-in-law and the lines are by the novelist himself.

See also THE WOLVERCOTE TONGUE.

JOHN RADCLIFFE HOSPITAL (JR2)

See RADCLIFFE INFIRMARY AND THE JOHN RADCLIFFE HOSPITAL (JR2).

· K ·

KIDLINGTON

This 'dormitory satellite' a few miles to the north of Oxford on the Banbury Road is the site of Thames Valley Police Headquarters. This, then, is where Morse's office is, though it is a faceless, barely described place in the novels. On screen, it has had three different incarnations, each many miles from Oxford. For the first two series a Territorial Army Centre in Southall, to the west of London, was used; in the third, fourth and fifth series the unit moved to another TA building, this time in Harrow; and for series six and seven an old Ministry of Defence laboratory was used.

Crime happens right on the CID's doorstep in *Death is Now My Neighbour*, for Kidlington is the location of the tidy little residential Bloxham Drive, where two murders occur in adjoining houses.

The neat little road in Kidlington visited by double murder in Death is Now My Neighbour.

· L ·

LANGUAGES, FOREIGN

Given his apparent insularity, Morse's knowledge of foreign languages seems surprising. He exercises his German on two occasions. The first is in *Who Killed Harry Field?*, when he says threateningly to the silent Carl, associate of the villain Paul Eirl, 'Du wirst mir antworten. Das kommt auf dich an.' (You will answer me. You must.) And in the film of *The Daughters of Cain*, to let 'Kay Bach' know that he knows she is really Kay Brooks, he murmurs, '*Sie sind nicht Kay Bach heute?*' (You are not Kay Bach today?)

Morse also knows the other 'operatic' language, Italian, and during his trip to Italy with Lewis in *The Death of the Self* gets considerable pleasure from speaking and hearing it. In *Last Seen Wearing*: 36 he also shows a working knowledge of French when testing Mrs Acum's own fluency in the language – though in fact earlier, in Chapter 7, 'he had always felt that a language which sanctioned the pronunciation of *donne, donnes* and *donnent* without the slightest differentiation could hardly deserve to be taken seriously'.

Morse has no knowledge of modern Greek – though he studied the ancient variety – and it is Lewis who scores here. His wife is a Greek speaker – she translates at a Cyprus sherry festival on one occasion – and in *Greeks Bearing Gifts* Lewis reveals that he has just started a modern Greek course. But when they find themselves interrogating two Greek witnesses who speak no English, Lewis feels at a loss: 'I can say it's a nice day and ask them if they sell beer. That's about it.'

LAST BUS TO WOODSTOCK (novel, 1975)

Sylvia Kaye, an Oxford office worker, is found murdered in the car park of the Black Prince public house at WOODSTOCK. Morse, teaming up with Lewis for the first time, is delighted to be in early possession of a cryptic clue: a bogus letter sent to Jennifer Coleby, one of Sylvia's colleagues at work. Alerted, but also distracted, by the bad spelling and poor standard of grammar in the typewritten letter, Morse does not immediately tumble to the fact that it is in code. But when he does, the solution is child's play for an old CROSSWORD buff like himself: concealed in the spelling mistakes is the message, 'SAY NOTHING'.

Morse is soon drawn into the lives of Jennifer and her two flatmates. In fact, he comes close to finding himself in love with one of them, twenty-three-year-old nurse Sue Widdowson, who, in turn, undoubtedly falls for his own particular brand of melancholic charm. But it is axiomatic that, for Morse, the course of true love has not the remotest chance of running smooth and after a single date Sue tells him of her engagement to a nice metallurgist called David. Much later, he will also uncover her concurrent affair with a married Oxford don.

This is Bernard Crowther, Fellow of LONSDALE COLLEGE. His appearance in the story initiates another important principle in the world of Morse, which is that the sordid, dubious or otherwise extracurricular activities of Oxford University dons can rarely be kept for long out of a Morse case. In fact, it is Crowther who has written the coded letter and he too picked up the hitchhiking victim, took her to Woodstock and had swift sex with her in the pub car park before she died.

Morse enthusiastically pursues several wrong hypotheses until Crowther's neurotic wife puts her head in the gas oven and the case suddenly unravels. No longer evading the consequences of his actions but seeking to atone for them, the don admits to Sylvia's murder. Almost at once, Morse is forced to doubt this confession by the arrival in the post of Mrs Crowther's suicide note, which contains a counter-confession. She claims she followed her husband to Woodstock and bludgeoned Sylvia to death herself. But the truth, as Morse now already knows, is different. He sums it up to a puzzled Lewis: 'All along, the trouble with this case has been not so much that they've been telling us downright lies but that they've told us such a tricky combination of lies and the truth.'

From this farrago of desire, jealousy, betrayal and mendacity comes nemesis for Crowther, in the shape of a fatal heart attack, and the ruin of Morse's romantic yearnings for Sue Widdowson. As he at last takes the real murderer into custody, he is forced to face the fact that his ROMANCE had been doomed from the start.

LAST BUS TO WOODSTOCK (TV film)

The crucial difference between this and Dexter's novel lies in the nature of the death of the girl, now called Sylvia Kane, in the WOODSTOCK pub – renamed the Fox and Castle. But the complex of relationships and motives remains substantially the same. So, although Sylvia's death in the film is not murder at all, but an accident which *looks* like murder, it is brought about by exactly the sort of passions which might have led to murder. As Crowther, the guilt-ridden LONSDALE COLLEGE don, says in his lecture on the poet and rake Lord Rochester, who died at Woodstock in 1680, 'The struggle of unsatisfied lust. Man's capacity for violence. That's something that urges on a man to rape, to kill even – murder. A madness that seizes the mind and drives out reason. Guilt? That comes later . . .'

Fabia Drake as Mrs Jarman in Last Bus to Woodstock.

First transmission 22 March 1988
Writer Michael Wilcox
Director Peter Duffell
Cast includes Anthony Bate, Fabia Drake, Terrence Hardiman

'LAST CALL' (short story, 1993)

It doesn't take Morse and Lewis long to construct a working hypothesis for the death in Room 231 at the RANDOLPH HOTEL. Peter Sherwood, a diabetic businessman attending a conference in Oxford, was found lying on the floor shortly after checking in. Dr HOBSON does not suspect violence and her decision is a massive heart attack at 6 p.m., just before Sherwood could give himself the second of his daily insulin injections. From the outset Morse is sure that Sherwood was accompanied by a mistress on this trip, although there is no trace of the woman herself. Perhaps she called for help on the internal phone and fled with her suitcase before anyone came. But then why, when they interview her, does Mrs Sherwood lie to Morse? Is it because she is a trained chemist and could have easily obtained the fatal substance that, on further analysis, Dr Hobson had found in her husband's insulin? Morse soon extracts a confession of intended murder from Mrs Sherwood. But it is the mistress he suspects of being ultimately responsible, for Morse now knows with all the certainty of his formidable intuition that it was love – or at least the anticipated excitement of sex – that killed Peter Sherwood.

LAST ENEMY, THE (TV film only)

TV film loosely based on the plot of the novel *The Riddle of the Third Mile*, but with significant changes. LONSDALE COLLEGE becomes BEAUMONT and the competition between the two college Fellows (here Drysdale and Kerridge) is not for the Mastership but for a prestigious lectureship which neither of them gets. Meanwhile, the Master himself, Sir Alexander Reece, is thwarted in his ambition to chair an important Royal Commission – 'a certain route to a peerage if you come up with the right conclusions', as Morse cynically puts it. The body pulled from the canal at Thrupp is as headless and limbless as in *The Riddle of the Third Mile* but its identity is different. Morse is at first misled into putting Reece into the frame as his chief suspect – until the Master too is shot dead and Morse is forced to look elsewhere for the murderer.

Many classic Morse themes are interwoven into this episode. There is a strong sense of the fatal hubris built into university life, the abiding and oh so fallible sense of its own superiority which Dexter calls the OXFORD DISEASE. And there is also the more universal preoccupation with the abuse of power – financial, political and sexual – running at some level through every episode. Above all, Morse himself is never more clearly adrift than here between the bright world of modern policing, with its computerized, scientific pragmatism, and his own archaic, cerebral concerns for true justice and philosophic wisdom.

First transmission 11 January 1989
Writer Peter Buckman, based on a story by Colin Dexter
Director James Scott
Cast includes Michael Aldridge, Tenniel Evans, Barry Foster, Sian Thomas.

LAST SEEN WEARING (novel, 1978)

'The case is cold now, sir – you must know that. People forget. Some people need to forget. Two years is a long time.'

'Two years, three months and two days,' corrected Strange. (*Last Seen Wearing*: 1)

The second Morse novel deals with what happens when an old, unsolved case suddenly wakes up in CID records and shakes its file at the police. Two years previously, a fifteen-year-old schoolgirl called Valerie Taylor had disappeared from the ROGER BACON COMPREHENSIVE SCHOOL during her lunch hour. With no body and no clues, the police have shelved the file, but now a brief letter of reassurance, apparently written by Valerie to her parents, has arrived out of the blue. As his remarks to Chief Superintendent STRANGE indicate, Morse is reluctant to take the case. But suddenly it comes to him that, from the first, this was never a missing-person but a murder inquiry: 'It's hard enough hiding a dead body, but it's a hell of a sight harder hiding a living one. I mean, a living one gets up and walks around and meets other people, doesn't it?' (1)

Once Morse gets an idea like this into his head, it's the devil's own job to shake it loose. Throughout the novel he goes several rounds in lively debate with Lewis, who is equally sure that Valerie is alive and that she, not her killer, wrote the letter.

Several of the principal characters are connected with secondary school EDUCATION. The French master, David Acum, is clever but a low-achiever in teaching. PHILLIPSON, the nervous, pernickety head, is in his mid-thirties and paying dearly for a single lapse from the highly moral standards of behaviour expected of a secondary school head. His deputy, Baines, is a nasty piece of work. Petty-minded, bitter and vindictive about not getting the headship himself, he is also a blackmailer. Like many of Dexter's murder victims, it doesn't seem entirely wrong – least of all to Morse – when he is found with a nine-inch kitchen knife plunged into his back.

Like the football-pools entry he vainly checks in Chapter 5, Morse generates an increasingly far-fetched sequence of permutations to solve the linked mysteries of Baines's murder and the fate of Valerie Taylor. As an inveterate CROSSWORD-puzzler, he shuffles the suspects and possibilities like letters in an anagram until he finds a workable conformation. But this case throws up several feasible hypotheses and, as each one is embraced

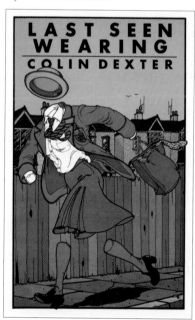

First editions of the early Morse novels in their dust jacket are worth serious money – particularly this one, which won a design prize.

and discarded, his mood swings from the bullish to the morose with increasing sharpness.

Despite Morse's frequent rudeness and unpredictability, he ends up smelling of roses. And not for the last time in his CID career one character – the headmaster's wife – stands, in the Epilogue, in awe of his preternatural powers:

> She would write, she decided, a long, long letter to Morse, and try to thank him from the bottom of her heart. For on that terrible evening it had been Morse who had found Donald and brought him to her; it had been Morse who had seemed to know and understand all things about them both . . .

Morse and Lewis are shown around Homewood School by Cheryl Baines in the film of Last Seen Wearing.

LAST SEEN WEARING (TV film)

Although two of the fundamental premises – the long-unsolved mystery of a disappearing schoolgirl and a head teacher with a sexual secret – are retained, the screen version of this story makes significant changes to Dexter's story. The comprehensive school is now a smart private girls' school; Mr Baines, the deputy head, is Miss Baines; the missing teenager, Valerie, no longer the daughter of a dustman, has a millionaire father who happens to sit on the Police Committee; and the unsavoury secrets of the school are presided over by an owner-headmaster, Donald PHILLIPSON. Peter McEnery brings to this role a huge relish for the nuances of neurotic male chauvinism.

First transmission 8 March 1988
Writer Thomas Ellice
Director Edward Bennett
Cast includes Suzanne Bertish, Glyn Houston, Peter McEnery, Frances Tomelty

LEWIS, SERGEANT ROBBIE

Lewis's past is known only in fragments. He is a Geordie, Newcastle-born. Leaving school at fifteen, he had avoided the seemingly inevitable lifetime of employment in a local engineering works, by 'working his way up through a series of day-release courses and demanding sessions at night schools to a fair level of competence in several technical skills' (*The Dead of Jericho*: 22). He spent a short while in the army, where he was a useful light-middleweight boxer. When he came out, the police force seemed a logical progression. He is married to a Welsh woman, Valerie Venables, and they have two children, Ken and Lyn. Lewis is an exceptionally decent man, with only two noticeable vices, the love of chips and fast driving. Otherwise he is the salt

Lewis: Morse's 'straight man'.

of the earth, with nothing remarkable about him: hard-working, 'the usual' Christian beliefs, anxious to better himself and to give his children a decent start in life.

Lewis plays a classic role in crime fiction. As the great detective's foil and sidekick, he is essentially a straight man – a counterpart who on the one hand is dull enough to allow the other's genius to shine out, and on the other possesses enough common sense and traditional wisdom to call the divinely inspired superman back to reality. This is the eternal role of men like Sherlock Holmes's Dr Watson, Hercule Poirot's Colonel Hastings and Lord Peter Wimsey's butler Bunter. But such individuals have a practical function too. They are there to serve – to do the legwork, carry the gun, drive the car, collar the suspect and (in Lewis's case) buy the drinks.

Lewis cannot be much of a brain – 'I envy blokes that work with their hands' (*Second Time Around*) – though he makes up for this with dedication and loyalty. Stalwartness and hero-worship have their limits, however, and Lewis is by no means uncritical of his boss. *Last Seen Wearing*: 14 shows Morse through Lewis's eyes as a flawed genius who 'always had to find a complex solution' when most crime, as Lewis well knew, derived from 'simple, cheap and sordid motives': 'What the great man couldn't do, for all his gifts, was put a couple of simple facts together and come up with something obvious.'

In *The Riddle of the Third Mile*: 24, Lewis is asked if Morse is a nice man.

'Well, I wouldn't exactly call him "nice".'

'Do you like him?'

'I don't think you "like" Morse. He's not that sort of person, really.'

What Lewis is struggling to convey here is that he doesn't *like* Morse, he *loves* him. However, in relation to Morse, Lewis is always subordinate. Morse is forever trying to improve Lewis's mind, or at least his grammar ('You'll never get on, Lewis, until you have mastered your sub-junctives'), while at the same time despairing of his intellectual clumsiness. A very funny instance of this is in *The Infernal Serpent*. The Master of Beaufort's wife is chatting idly with Morse about her reputation as a high-quality piano teacher, when Lewis suddenly interjects, mischievously or otherwise, 'I bought my nippers one of them electronic keyboards, meself…' Lewis – with more than a hint of mockery – is playing up to the role of the philistine. But it is gaffes like these that enable Morse to maintain his sense of superiority over Lewis, as if his Sergeant were a stereotypically pre-feminist wife, floundering to keep up with her husband's effortless mastery of CULTURE and ideas. Indeed, Lewis is, in many ways, Morse's surrogate wife. Their relationship is very like a parody of a particularly old-fashioned marriage.

He's driving: Morse and Lewis in characteristic formation in The Dead of Jericho.

The occasions when Lewis is solicitous and protective towards Morse are many. Morse trusts Lewis with the key to his flat. Lewis brings him pyjamas in hospital, explains the intricacies of baby-care to him, makes him take his medicine, and keeps vigil outside the flat after Morse's grand passion, Susan Fallon, has killed herself.

But there are rows too, the most dramatic and interesting of which is in the film version of *The Way Through the Woods*. Unable to contain himself after years of bottled-up frustration, the ever-placid Lewis suddenly loses his temper. Morse, who has persistently bullied and belittled him, now finds himself facing the possibility that his sergeant is going to leave him for an inspector's job with the Regional Crime Squad, all at the prompting of 'another man' – DCI Johnson. The shouting match which ensues is *exactly* like a marital row.

Lewis contemplating Masonic Mysteries.

> LEWIS: This was never about Johnson. This is about you and me.
> MORSE: *You* and *me*?
> LEWIS: Yes. I proved myself a decent detective, but you're such a bloody arrogant, self-centred bastard, you'd rather die than ever admit it.
> MORSE: I once thought you'd make a decent detective, Lewis. Given the right encouragement. But it seems you have neither the wit nor the imagination. In that respect, you and Johnson are a well-matched pair.
> LEWIS: Well, perhaps it's just as well I'm leaving, then, isn't it?
> MORSE: (*shocked*) What?

Of course, Lewis never does make the break, accepting instead his eternal subordination to Morse. For Morse, this is lucky, because his sergeant is 'the catalytic factor in the curious chemistry of Morse's mind' (*The Way Through the Woods*: 44) and is, therefore, irreplaceable.

LEWIS, VALERIE

In the *Morse* films, Lewis's wife (played by Maureen Bennett) speaks only once, during a Greek-restaurant scene in *Greeks Bearing Gifts*, when she orders the food for Lewis and herself. Although she does this in English, it appears from the following exchange in *Cherubim and Seraphim* that she is fluent in modern Greek:

LEWIS: Where's Mam?

SON: Down the wine shop. Translating. It's Cyprus sherry week.

She also appears, without speaking (either in English or Greek), in *Fat Chance* and *Masonic Mysteries*.

LITERATURE

Morse is a reader. His flat is described in 'As Good As Gold' as 'book-lined' and in the novel *The Dead of Jericho* we find him attending meetings of the Oxford Book Association. Beside his bed in the novel *Last Seen Wearing* are found John Livingston Lowes's study of the poet Coleridge, *The Road to Xanadu*, *A Selection of Kipling's Short Stories*, *The Life of Richard Wagner* by Ernest Newman and *The Selected Prose of A. E. Housman*.

It's not surprising that the Lewises don't enjoy dinner at their local Greek restaurant – the chef has been murdered.

Dexter writes, 'Morse was not a systematic reader; he was a dipper-in' (18). But once he *had* been – escaping into books from a miserable, some-time suicidal, adolescence. Like a true reader, his mind is haunted by books and literary analogies. In the novel *The Way Through the Woods* he looks out to sea at Lyme Regis and 'tells himself he must re-read *The Odyssey*' (4) once again. In the same novel he travels to Ottery St Mary to seek out traces of Coleridge and is disappointed at what little remains.

If searching a room which happens to be a murder scene, in Colin Dexter's work Morse is always liable to be distracted by a book he finds there – Robert Louis Stevenson's *Travels with a Donkey* in *Last Seen Wearing*, the poetry of Andrew Marvell in *The Silent World of Nicholas Quinn*, Catullus in *The Daughters of Cain*, *Topless in Torremolinos* in *Death is Now My Neighbour*, *The Collected Poems of Housman* in 'The Inside Story'.

Poetry is his greatest love. In the novel *The Dead of Jericho*: 2 we find him attending a meeting of the

Kipling, revered by Morse for his understanding of women.

Oxford Book Association, which is being addressed by a great literary scholar, Professor Dame Helen Gardner, on the subject of her *New Oxford Book of English Verse*. Morse is 'caught up in the spontaneous appreciation' which her scholarship and sensitivity evoked in the audience, and

> he earnestly resolved that he would make an immediate attempt to come to terms with the complexities of the *Four Quartets*. He ought, he knew, to come along more often to talks such as these; keep his mind fresh and sharp – a mind so often dulled these days by cigarettes and alcohol. Surely that's what life was all about? Opening doors; opening doors and peering through them – perhaps even finding the rose gardens there . . .'.

Another great literary attachment – probably his greatest – is to the works of A. E. Housman, the poet and Professor of Latin whose elegiac verse meditations sing in such close harmony with Morse's own individual brand of nostalgic melancholy. Francis Thompson, Housman's exact contemporary (both were born in 1859), is another admired poet and in *The Last Enemy* Morse caps his old tutor's quotation from *The Hound of Heaven* with another from the same source. Morse is also familiar with the most monumental of all the Victorian poets – not initially out of free choice, as we discover in the TV version of *Death is Now My Neighbour*. When Morse intones those stirring lines about old age from *Ulysses* which end 'To strive, to seek, to find and not to yield', Strange is disconcerted:

STRANGE: Are you all right, Morse?

MORSE: Tennyson, sir. My father made me learn it by heart.

In prose, the Victorians also rate highly in Morse's estimation. Every Christmas he reads – or rather re-reads – a Dickens novel. When in 'As Good As Gold' Lewis asks him for some advice about the best ones, he replies, 'I'd put *Bleak House* first, *Little Dorrit* second.'

His second favourite novelist is Hardy – whose country he is found exploring while feeling pangs of nostalgia in *The Way Through the Woods*: 16 – but his favourite short story is Kipling's 'Love o' Women', which he discusses with Sheila Williams in *The Jewel That Was Ours*: 24. In fact Morse, 'firmly believed that Kipling knew more about women than Kinsey ever had' (*Last Seen Wearing: 18*).

Despite his sheepish enjoyment of PORNOGRAPHY, Morse is generally scornful of contemporary lowbrow fiction, such as that produced by May Lawrence, the murdered novelist in *The Death of the Self*. He has 'always enjoyed Agatha Christie', however.

Even in his serious reading he has a taste for puckish humour. For example, one of his favourite quotations comes from the historian of *The Decline and Fall of the Roman Empire*, Edward Gibbon, which Morse memorized as a boy. It concerns a Renaissance Pope: 'The most scandalous charges were suppressed; the vicar of Christ was only accused of piracy, murder, rape, sodomy and incest.'

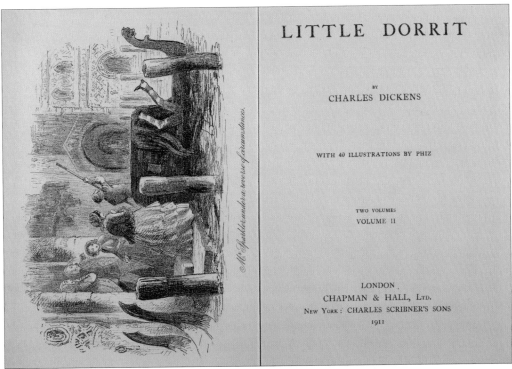

The title page of Dickens' Little Dorrit, *illustrated by Phiz in the 1911 edition.*

LONSDALE COLLEGE

Although in the books Morse was an undergraduate at St John's, in *Deceived by Flight* he is described by Roland Marshall as 'a Lonsdale man'. Even if Marshall's memory is playing him false, Lonsdale is undoubtedly the Oxford college Morse has come to know best since joining the police force. He has few illusions about the saintliness, or even good behaviour, of the members of the university as a whole ('And, gentlemen, what a hole Oxford is!' as the Master of Lonsdale himself remarks to the assembled foreign students in *The Settling of the Sun* as Morse, sitting beside him, groans at the frequently heard joke). But Lonsdale, it would appear, is in a class of its own for the excesses of deadly sinfulness practised inside its ancient precincts.

Filming The Way Through the Woods, *with Brasenose as Lonsdale.*

Lonsdale is essentially an amalgam, Dexter's cipher for the Oxford colleges in general. It is based, however, on BRASENOSE.

Not every misdeed committed in the world of Morse happens at or around Lonsdale, but the college harbours a disturbing concentration of crime. The list of dubious dons dining in college is a long one, beginning with the murder suspect in *Last Bus to Woodstock*, Dr Bernard Crowther, continuing via the neurotic Dr Jane Robson in *The Settling of the Sun* and the porn addict Dr Alan Hardinge in *The Way Through the Woods*, to the murderous Dr and Mrs Storrs in *Death is Now My Neighbour*. Nor is the quality of college leadership all that it might be. If the Master in *The Settling of the Sun*, Sir Wilfrid Mulryne, is a confirmed cynic and womanizer, he is outdone by his successor later in the series, Sir Clixby Bream, who is both these things and a blackmailer to boot. Meanwhile, in *The Day of the Devil* Bursar Willowbank's depravity runs as far as a sincere belief in Satanism.

At the beginning of *The Way Through the Woods* Morse attends a concert at Lonsdale and gallantly buys a programme for Claire Osborne – the start of yet another doomed ROMANCE.

· M ·

McNutt, Desmond

Named after D. S. McNutt, Ximenes crossword setter, this man was an inspiring Thames Valley Chief Inspector for whom Morse had once worked. In *Masonic Mysteries* Morse and Lewis drive out to see McNutt, who, since taking early retirement, had moved to Reading and become a clergyman. McNutt, says Morse, 'taught me everything I know'. His particular strength is his psychological insight: '[he] looked right inside people's minds. Their souls.'

McNutt's good and useful life ends when Hugo de Vries kills him, as part of his campaign of persecution against Morse. The body is hidden in Morse's flat.

Magdalen College

This is the college whose bell-tower is one of the greatest landmarks in Oxford. From here May Day is celebrated when the college choir sings the hymn to spring, *Te Deum Patrem Colimus*. The college is featured in the films *The Dead of Jericho*, *Dead on Time* and *Twilight of the Gods*.

Mail, Oxford

Oxford's best-known local newspaper (there are also the *Oxford Times* and the *Oxford Chronicle*) is published by the Oxford and Cowley Press (The 'Ox and Cow'). It is several times used by Morse to push along a stalled inquiry – for instance, in *Last Bus to Woodstock*: 19, *The Silent World of Nicholas Quinn*: 13 and *The Riddle of the Third Mile*: 16. In the latter case he dictates over the phone an entirely misleading piece about the dismembered murder victim's socks, which he says are from Marks and Spencer. In reality, Morse does not even have the corpse's feet, let

Magdalen tower, seen from the Botanic Gardens.

alone its socks. His article is intended to convince the murderer that the police know more than they do – a bluff which, in fact, has precisely the opposite effect. In any event, the helpful editor seems happy enough to print Morse's highly tendentious 'journalism'.

In *Death is Now My Neighbour* the suspect and subsequent murder victim Geoffrey Owens is a journalist at the *Mail*.

MARKET, COVERED

Lying between the High and Market Street, this is a busy warren of passageways lined by small shops selling fresh produce and manufactured goods, as well as cafés and sandwich shops. One of Britain's oldest covered markets, it dates back to 1773. In *Greeks Bearing Gifts*, Maria comes here with Jocasta Georgiadis, only to give her minder the slip and run off through the crowds. Maria is not seen again until she turns up floating in the Isis. In *Absolute Conviction*, the murderer out of jail, Bennett, runs through the market to escape Lewis and Morse.

MARRIAGE

In *Deceived by Flight* Anthony Donn asks Morse if he minds not being married: 'Sometimes I mind,' he replies. In *Driven to Distraction* he tells Detective Sergeant Maitland, 'My mother used to say that priests should be married – what do they understand if they won't marry? Maybe the same is true about policemen.' But it is hard to imagine Morse married. In *Dead on Time* we learn he was once engaged to Susan Bryce-Morgan, but she left him for Henry Fallon and the experience left a permanent emotional scar. But despite this, he has clearly had his offers. In *The Secret of Bay 5B*, he tells the prostitute Camilla that he has been 'too choosy, too hesitant, too lazy, too busy . . .' to marry. The most compelling reason may be his wariness of an institution which had gone so disastrously wrong in the case of his own parents. 'Matrimony is a bargain, and somebody has to get the worst of the bargain', in the words of Helen Rowland, quoted at the head of *The Secret of Annexe 3*: 41. This means, for Morse, that it may also be a gamble and – as we know – he has given up GAMBLING.

A wife for Morse would in any case be hard to find in today's world. First, it would be unthinkable for Morse to marry a woman who was cleverer than himself. Then she would have to be unquestionably loyal, have a skin as thick as a rhinoceros, be energetic, practical, patient and tolerant – and pay for all his drinks. But, as pointed out elsewhere, there is someone already playing this role in his life: the precondition of marriage for Morse would be a divorce from Sergeant Lewis.

In March 1998 there was speculation in the press that the absence of Lewis from the forthcoming film version of *The Wench is Dead* would indeed open the way for Morse to marry. However, Colin Dexter, when approached by the *Mail on Sunday*, was adamant that he would not allow this: 'The whole point about Morse is that he is a man of independence. He has a bottle of Scotch in his bottom right-hand drawer for company and he never needs to explain or apologize to anyone.' (*See also* 'Foreword'.)

Carlton have also denied this (*see also* WENCH IS DEAD, THE).

MARSTON

In this village on the eastern fringes of Oxford Morse goes for a drink with Kay Brooks in the film *The Daughters of Cain*.

MASONIC MYSTERIES (TV film only)

Morse's amateur choir is taking part in a performance of Mozart's *The Magic Flute* when the dress rehearsal is interrupted by the murder of Beryl Newsome, a woman for whom he has recently developed a fancy. Found with knife in hand cradling the dead Beryl, Morse becomes suspect number one for Chief Inspector Bottomley, whom STRANGE has put in charge of the case. It is the beginning of a nightmare-parody of the opera's plot, as Morse is put through a series of 'trials', modern versions of the ordeals by darkness, silence, fire and water undergone by Tamino in the opera. They are orchestrated by Hugo de Vries, an evil

Ordeal by fire: Morse's flat blazing in Masonic Mysteries.

genius of a confidence trickster put away by Morse in the distant days when he was an 'ignorant sergeant' working under Chief Inspector Desmond MCNUTT. De Vries, now at liberty, 'doesn't want my death but my hurt. My disgrace. My complete public humiliation!'

Before long £100,000 is stolen from a charity and turns up in Morse's account. Then the bloody corpse of McNutt himself, Morse's old mentor and, for Morse, a man of surpassing wisdom, like the opera's high priest Sorastro, is found hidden in Morse's flat. Finally Morse, when his flat is fire-bombed, is almost burned to death, and his record collection is completely destroyed.

Despite its dark shades, the film is also full of comedy. Much fun is made here of Bottomley's membership of the lodge – FREEMASONRY in the force being a topical subject in 1990. And, when it is discovered that de Vries's firebomb is contrived from an audio cassette of *The Magic Flute*, Morse's musical sensibility is even more pained than his body when he realizes it is a version conducted by Arturo Toscanini: 'Talk about adding insult to injury. That's the worst recording of *The Magic Flute* ever made! I wouldn't allow it in the *house*.'

First transmission 24 January 1990
Writer Julian Mitchell
Director Danny Boyle
Cast includes Iain Cuthbertson, Diane Fletcher, Ian McDiarmid

MERTON COLLEGE

The Fellows' Garden of this college, on Merton Street, was used for garden scenes in *The Infernal Serpent*.

MODERN LIFE

Morse lives at some psychological distance from the modern world, dating this dislocation to the 1960s: 'I missed the '60s, Lewis. I was based at Windsor when the Rolling Stones played on Eel Pie Island. I was just never in the right place at the right time' (*Cherubim and Seraphim*).

Since those days, matters have become much worse. Morse refuses to drive – or think in – a car that is not 'pre-electrics'. He does not own a television ('What is this modern compulsion to entertain unknown millions with your closest secrets?' – *Greeks Bearing Gifts*) but loves the radio. He is terrified of technology:

The Fellows' Garden: Merton as it appears in The Infernal Serpent.

MORSE: I hate answer machines.

LEWIS: That's because you know all the answers.

And on word processors and computers (from *The Last Enemy*):

LEWIS: You always knock 'em, sir. But if you knew how to get them to tell you what you want . . .

DR RUSSELL: I still prefer a pen.

MORSE: So do I. One with a nib that you fill from a bottle.

'Boys' games,' George Linacre tells Morse when, in *The Sins of the Fathers*, they remember their mutual long-ago undergraduate interest in real ale. 'It's a competitive world out there now.' In many ways, Morse's oddity is that, unlike Linacre, he has become stuck in those old student days. A similar problem afflicts the murderer Victor Preece in the same film, looked after by his mother as he plays with his model railway. Morse's interests, however, are not childish. They are those of a particular kind of adolescent or very young man – puzzles, word play, PORNOGRAPHY, romantic MUSIC, intellectual competitiveness. Since it was in the late 1940s and 1950s that he passed through this stage, his dominant tastes and tendencies, his CAR and his music, belong to that era.

Morse is too proud – or arrogant – to have truck with modern technology or to update his attitudes about FEMINISM, DRUGS and LITERATURE. His favourite modern poet is Philip Larkin. In grey twill trousers and a tweed sports jacket, Larkin was above all the bard of beer and of brooding disappointment; a man who harboured an 'innocent' taste for pornography and who ruefully watched the sexual revolution happening in the 1960s, 'too late for me'. All of which is Morse to a tee.

MONEY

Morse generally shows little respect for money. He despises wealth and has no serious interest in the luxuries that it can buy. Yet he is shamelessly parsimonious, always expecting Lewis to stand him drinks and stamp his letters without hope of recompense.

Meanness is a symptom of psychological insecurity and can usually be traced back to childhood trauma. The break-up of his parents' marriage is therefore probably the key to this, Morse's least forgivable weakness, as it is to so much else about him. With an effort, he can overcome the tendency. After a tussle with himself, he gives money to McNutt's tramp in *Masonic Mysteries*, he buys two dozen roses for the opera singer Gwladys Probert in *Twilight of the Gods* and, one Christmas in the story 'Morse's Greatest Mystery', he even makes good, out of his own pocket, the stolen £400 collected by the George public house for a children's charity. Later in this story he feels a sense of enlightenment. If the greatest mystery is what makes happiness, perhaps he has at last solved it: perhaps the answer is generosity.

MORSE, CHIEF INSPECTOR ENDEAVOUR

Colin Dexter says that, as a writer, his interest is in the puzzle and not in the characters. But, well constructed though his plots are, it is the puzzle of Morse's personality which makes his tales stand out.

From fragments and hints scattered throughout the canon, the outlines of Morse's biography can be pieced together. He was born towards the end of September 1930, in Stamford, Lincolnshire. His father, a taxi driver, had an obsession with Captain Cook, and his mother, 'a gentle soul' who nevertheless instilled in her son a respect for hard work, was a Quaker. Out of this combination of commitments in each of his parents came the embarrassing peculiarity of Morse's Christian name, which he would go through life trying to conceal: Endeavour.

Academically Morse did well, progressing easily to the grammar school, but then, almost immediately, his father left, upping and marrying his 'fancy woman', Gwen. Among the painful revelations made by Morse to Lewis in the film *Cherubim and Seraphim* are that his mother died when he was fifteen and the boy reluctantly moved in with his father and stepmother, who by now had given birth to a child of her own, Joyce.

Morse takes time to think in The Silent World of Nicholas Quinn. *But is he musing on life and death, or trying to crack 1 down in* The Times *crossword?*

After briefly considering suicide, Morse found that reading and schoolwork took his mind off his unhappiness at home. There was a long-lasting ROMANCE with a girl at the grammar school which ended when he went up for National Service at the age of eighteen.

His eighteen-month army career in the Royal Signals Regiment was unmemorable – though he would carry to the end of his days the itchy discomfort of battledress. When it was finished he went up with a scholarship to St John's College, Oxford, to read classics and, refusing to reveal the name he had been christened with, was nicknamed 'Pagan'. He studied with enthusiasm until half-way through his third year, when he found himself in love with a postgraduate student at St Hilda's, Wendy Spencer. Morse fell for Wendy with everything he'd got but the end of their passionate affair a year later had a disastrous effect on his academic work and he went down from Oxford having failed the classics degree, known as Greats. Morse was now 'a withdrawn and silent young man, bitterly belittled, yet not completely broken in spirit. It had been his sadly disappointed old father, a month or so before his death, who suggested that his only son might find a niche in the police force' (*The Riddle of the Third Mile*: 7).

Morse's psyche swarms with neuroses. His compulsive temperament was inherited from his father (that obsession with Cook is very revealing) and his melancholia, perhaps from his mother. But the origin of his PHOBIAS and pedantry, his alternating assertiveness and self-doubt, love of puzzles and butterfly mind is anybody's guess.

So is the source of his attractiveness for women. Why this tetchy, middle-aged policeman should have women swooning at the merest whiff of his pheromones is a mystery, though it seems he possesses an enviable ability to make women feel understood:

> She thought of Morse, and she felt inexpressively glad that she had met him; longed, too, with one half of her mind, that he would come to visit her again. And yet she knew, quite certainly, that if he did her soul would be completely bared and she would tell him all she knew. (*The Riddle of the Third Mile*: 29)

Another woman has the same feeling, though she expresses it more sexually: 'She felt a strong compulsion about the man. It was not so much that he seemed mentally to be undressing her, as most of the men she knew, as if he had already done so.' (*Last Bus to Woodstock*: 2)

Happiness is not something Morse finds easily. Work makes him happy and therefore murder, more than anything, cheers him. But it also satisfies his passion for truth and his sense, although it is often unorthodox, of justice.

Morse has few friends and those he does have are not necessarily attractive, at least on the surface. He likes difficulty and challenge, spitting defiance whenever he senses the offer of an easy way through. Like Sherlock Holmes, leisure and jollification have no appeal for him because he sees himself as a protagonist of tragic events and thrives only because of them.

See also 'Foreword'.

Morse's mind is a finely tuned instrument but his heart is forever playing out of tune. The final scene of Death is Now My Neighbour *shows him walking, at last, into a happy ending!*

'MORSE'S GREATEST MYSTERY' (short story, 1987)

Morse, on leave over the Christmas holidays, is far from content when Lewis calls on him.

> 'I don't like Christmas – never have.'
> 'You staying in Oxford, sir?'
> 'I'm going to decorate.'
> 'What – decorate the Christmas cake?'
> 'Decorate the kitchen. I don't like Christmas cake – never did.'
> 'You get more like Scrooge every minute, sir.'

Scrooge-like, then, Morse is called to a pub where a charity collection for children has been stolen and, his conscience mildly stricken, he manages by mysterious sleight of hand, and not a little injury to his own bank balance, to return the MONEY without explaining to a soul how he did it. His own strange sense of inner content is baffling to him after this: 'He had solved so many mysteries in his life. Was he now, he wondered, beginning to glimpse the solution to the greatest mystery of them all?'

MORSE'S LAW

The law concerns the likelihood of the person who has reported the discovery of a body being the murderer. In the film version of *The Silent World of Nicholas Quinn*, Morse states his law after they have inspected the remains of the poisoned Quinn. In the last scene, Lewis reminds him of it:

> LEWIS: We should have arrested Martin straight away.
> MORSE: Why?
> LEWIS: Morse's Law. You said there's always a fifty-fifty chance that whoever finds the body did the deed.

But by now the Chief Inspector has changed his tune.

> MORSE: That's not Morse's Law, Lewis. Morse's Law is, there's always time for one more pint.

MUSIC

Morse is very emotional about music. Records are his children; the concerts he goes to are imbued with holiness for him. In *The Settling of the Sun*, trying to talk to the child Alex Robson about her dead grandfather, he says: 'I knew him. We used to take him to concerts, your aunt and I, a few. I don't know whether he enjoyed them or not. He used to cry. I often cry at concerts. Do you?'

At the end of *The Death of the Self* we see him doing just that – weeping at the Verona amphitheatre as he listens to Nicole Burgess's Puccini aria (actually the voice of Janis

'The Welsh Canary': Gwladys Probert is in glass-shattering form for a masterclass attended by Morse in Twilight of the Gods.

Kelly). Music and poetry are the only spiritual sustenance Morse takes. In *Fat Chance*, he is asked by Emma Pickford whether he ever experiences so much as a glimmer of religious faith and he can only say, 'Sometimes when I'm listening to music . . .'

As a committed RADIO listener, Morse more than once mulls over the eight records he would choose if ever invited on to *Desert Island Discs* and it is possible to work out what at least some of his selections would be. He would certainly include the '*Recordare*' from Mozart's *Requiem* (in *The Way Through the Woods*: 48 he lists his five favourite recordings of this work). He would also have Richard Strauss's 'melismatic' *Vier Letzte Lieder*, Dvořák's *American Quartet* and the 'In Paradisum' from Fauré's *Requiem*. Probably the rest of the records would be WAGNER – especially from elements of *The Ring*, sung by Kirsten Flagstad or Gwladys Probert, 'the greatest diva of her time'.

On screen, Morse himself sings frequently, but only as a member of an ensemble. The second thing we see him do in the entire series is to arrive late for a practice after arresting some villains: he hurries in and sits down just in time to sing the final note. 'Are you the singing detective?' asks one character in the same episode. In *Masonic Mysteries* he is in the chorus for a performance of *The Magic Flute* by Mozart, wearing a preposterous masonic costume. In *The Infernal Serpent* we meet Jake Normington, the mathematician and musician whose 'Renaissance Group' once employed Morse's 'useful baritone'.

The screen Morse often goes to the opera – in Oxford and London, not to mention Bayreuth, Sydney and Verona. In *The Ghost in the Machine* this habit enables him to defeat Lady Hanbury's alibi since he was himself at Covent Garden for the performance of Puccini's *Tosca* which she pretends to have attended, not realizing that 'Domingo had a cold and couldn't sing'. In *The Wolvercote Tongue*, when we find him booking tickets for Berlioz's *The Trojans*, we appreciate that his tastes are not frivolous:

MORSE: Never, never interrupt me when I'm booking my seat for the opera, Lewis.

LEWIS: Sorry, sir.

MORSE: I might get *Madame Butterfly* instead of Berlioz; I might get Handel, for God's sake.

Barrington PHELOUNG's music plays an essential part in the TV films. The way the *Morse* theme plays the name 'Morse' in Morse Code, — —   — — —   • — •   ••• •, is a delightful cryptic touch, but it is not the only one. The scores are written after the film has been edited and assembled so that Pheloung is able to tailor the music to fit closely with the images – a Chinese instrument for a Whitehall mandarin in *The Last Enemy*, the letters of the villain's

name 'Eirl' in *Who Killed Harry Field?* and so on. All the music in the films is either composed or arranged by Pheloung and performed under his supervision. Two striking and contrasting examples are *The Magic Flute* for *Masonic Mysteries* – Pheloung arranged, conducted and recorded a third of the entire opera especially for the episode – and the lovely Brahms Sextet (in B major opus 18) heard in *The Day of the Devil*. His contributions to original music include Australian country and western songs in *Promised Land* and rhythm 'n' blues tracks for *Who Killed Harry Field?*

There have been several commercial recordings of the incidental music from the *Morse* soundtrack. *Inspector Morse*, Volumes 1–3 (issued 1991–2) are on the Virgin label, as is *The Essential Morse* (1995). *The Passion of Morse Suite*, composed and conducted by Barrington Pheloung with the Royal Philharmonic Orchestra, was issued in 1997 by Tring Records.

See also RADIO.

'Donner' – Arthur Rackham's vision of a Wagnerian hero.

'NEIGHBOURHOOD WATCH' (short story, 1992)

This story records one of the few occasions when Morse is comprehensively outsmarted. A casual acquaintance, Dr Eric Ullman, is regaling the Chief Inspector and a few others in the King's Arms with an odd story. His recently stolen car had, a few nights ago, reappeared in his driveway and the thief had left a note of apology tucked under the wiper. As a token of thanks he had included a free ticket, best in the house, for a forthcoming performance in Oxford of Wagner's *Die Walküre.*

Morse is sure the whole episode is a 'subtle strategy of deception' designed to get Ullman out of the house on the night of the performance. But he doesn't want to alarm him or spoil his enjoyment of the opera (which happens to be his own favourite, as well as the thief's, if the apologetic windscreen note is a truthful guide) – nor does he want to look a fool if he's wrong. So without telling its occupant, he and Lewis position themselves outside the Ullman home on the night in question to await developments.

But the deception is too subtle even for Morse and, while Dr Ullman is not the one burgled that night, our hero is almost left minus the one piece of valuable furniture in his own nearby flat: 'the family heirloom – nest of tables – Chippendale, 1756'. But thanks to Dr Ullman, who here plays a role akin to that of Sherlock Holmes's twice-as-clever brother, Mycroft, this sole relic of the Morse ancestors is preserved after all.

NEW COLLEGE

This very ancient college (it dates from 1379) lies on New College Lane. The service at the beginning of *Fat Chance* was filmed in its magnificent fourteenth-century chapel.

New and old: a scene in New College from Fat Chance.

The Old Parsonage Hotel, North Oxford.

NEWSPAPERS

While he scoffs at Lewis's attachment to the *Sunday* and *Daily Mirror*, one of Morse's own Sunday papers is always the *News of the World*. The *Observer* is equally essential to him, for it contains the Azed CROSSWORD, the successor to the celebrated Ximenes.

NORTH OXFORD

The area between the Banbury and the Woodstock roads is generally known as North Oxford. Here are many large Victorian properties built in a way John Ruskin would have approved of, in the 'Venetian Gothic' style charmingly described here by Dexter:

> Most of these houses (with their yellowish beige bricks and the purple blue slates of their roofs) may perhaps appear to the modern eye as rather severe and humourless. But such an assessment would be misleading: attractive bands of orange brick serve to soften the ecclesiastical discipline of many of these great houses, and over the arches the pointed contours are re-emphasized by patterns of orange and purple, as though the old harlot of the Mediterranean had painted on her eyeshadow a little too thickly. (*The Secret of Annexe 3*: 3)

One of these – though not the most 'Venetian' – is the OLD PARSONAGE HOTEL, on which *The Secret of Annexe 3*'s Haworth Hotel is based.

· O ·

OLD PARSONAGE HOTEL

This comfortable hotel in North Oxford, 'dating back to 1660', is the one in which Julia Stevens and Brenda Brooks lunch in *The Daughters of Cain*: 20 and where later (50) Morse meets Ellie Smith and treats her to an £18 half-bottle of champagne. The Haworth Hotel, scene of the murder in *The Secret of Annexe 3*, is loosely based on it.

OXFORD DISEASE, THE

There is in Oxford, according to Sheila Williams in *The Jewel That Was Ours*: 33, an endemic 'tragic malady which deludes its victims into believing they can never be wrong in any matter of knowledge or opinion'. In the film *The Last Enemy*, Deborah Burns has an even worse opinion of the Gown side of Oxford: 'A vicious, backbiting, petty-minded, parochial little town that thinks it's the centre of the universe'. Morse is later a little kinder as he construes the unreality of university life: 'Once you're taken to the university's bosom, Lewis, you're preserved like Sleeping Beauty in a rarefied atmosphere of hot air and alcohol. Ageing is unknown.'

The dons in Morse's world are different from the prim, fussy, anally-retentive types known in the past, such as W. H. Auden's don, who claimed, 'I don't feel quite happy about pleasure.' But they are certainly intensely political and spiteful. As Sir Clixby Bream, Master of Lonsdale, says in the TV version of *Death is Now My Neighbour* to Shelly Cornford, 'You're new to Oxford – you don't understand. The dons are malicious, spiteful creatures. They don't vote for someone, they vote against them. That's why they'll vote against Denis, even though he's the best man for the job . . . He's let them know how much he wants it.'

But despite the fog of petty political squabbling, financial woe and faltering academic standards, the ineffable superiority of Oxford will always shine through. In Gielgud's portrayal, University Chancellor Lord Hinksey is a wickedly funny embodiment of the Oxford Disease.

HINKSEY: We could have had the ceremony after all. God knows when you'll be a doctor now.
STANSKY: I *am* a doctor, Lord Hinksey.
HINKSEY: A medical doctor, yes. Easier to be a medical doctor. Just have to pass a few exams. But to get an *honorary* doctorate . . .
STANSKY: And I've got two of those already, as a matter of fact.
HINKSEY: I've got fifteen. Sixteen if you count Yale.
STANSKY: I'm *from* Yale.
HINKSEY: Well, there you are, then. American degrees are just two a penny.

Pomp and ceremony at the Bridge of Sighs. The Chancellor of the University processes to the Sheldonian Theatre for an honorary degree ceremony.

· P ·

PARK TOWN

This is a crucial setting in both the novel and the film of *The Way Through the Woods*. It is a Victorian development (1853–5) in NORTH OXFORD, consisting of two crescents of brick and stucco terraced houses in late classical style curving around a central garden. The rented house in which – as Morse discovers – pornographic photo sessions and a murder had taken place a year earlier is one of those on the southern crescent and called (fictionally) Seckham Villa, after the crescent's architect, Samuel Lipscomb Seckham.

PARSON'S PLEASURE

This well-known male bathing place on the River Cherwell is approached through the University Parks ('the setting for countless copulations since Royalist artillery was quartered on its acres during the civil war' – *The Jewel That Was Ours*: 19). Famous for the nude bathing that could be enjoyed there even in Victorian times, Parson's Pleasure seems a slyly appropriate place for the naked and waterlogged body of the philandering Dr Theodore Kemp to turn up, lodged on top of the weir.

Parson's Pleasure, c. 1913.

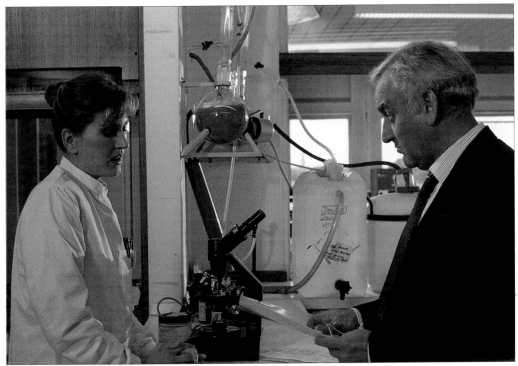

All Morse wants from a pathologist is a time of death – unless she happens to be attractive and single. Morse and Dr Russell in The Secret of Bay 5B.

PATHOLOGIST(S)

A detective specializing in murder requires a pathologist in just the way that a pilot needs a navigator. But while a pilot needs a direction to steer, what Morse wants above all from Max de BRYN, Grayling RUSSELL or Laura HOBSON when they examine the corpse is a time of death. The scenes in which he spars with the pathologists, trying to cut through the scientific flim-flam and get them to commit themselves, became a ritual from the moment the 'hump-backed surgeon' made his first anonymous appearance in *Last Seen Wearing*: 19. For the first two film series Peter Woodthorpe made an unforgettable impact as the pathologist Max de Bryn, until, in the third series, a new pathologist arrived, Dr Grayling Russell, played by Amanda Hillwood. The possibility of a ROMANCE between her and Morse teased us for four films, until it was time to try something fresh. Thereafter no one pathologist recurs until *The Daughters of Cain*, *The Way Through the Woods* and *Death is Now My Neighbour*, when Dr Laura Hobson (Clare Holman) comes on the scene to attract Morse with her sexy northern vowels.

All the pathologists involved in Morse cases are based at the William Dunn School of Pathology, the university's own Pathology Department, on South Parks Road. Scenes in many *Morse* films have been shot there.

PETERS

Dry, precise and unemotional, the handwriting expert Peters is a former Home Office pathologist. Morse consults him first in *Last Seen Wearing*: 10 over the 'three lines of drab uncultured scrawl', apparently sent to her parents by the missing Valerie Taylor. Peters is only 'ninety per cent sure' that the letter was written by Valerie, and Morse, desperate to show that Valerie is alive, decides to test the expert himself by forging a second letter, which in turn is submitted to Peters. The verdict is the same – a 90 per cent assurance.

Morse returns to Peters in *The Silent World of Nicholas Quinn*: 17 to solicit an opinion on the note Quinn appears to have left for his cleaner just before getting murdered. He knows only that 'if Peters said that Quinn had definitely written the note, Quinn had definitely written the note. If he said he wasn't sure, he wasn't sure; and no one else in the world would be sure.'

In this case Peters, inconveniently for Morse's current theory of the murder, is sure: 'Quinn wrote it.'

PHELOUNG, BARRINGTON

The musical director for all the *Morse* films is an astonishingly versatile and prolific Australian musician who arranges or composes, and frequently performs, all the *Morse* MUSIC. Even the choral pieces are Pheloung and a handful of friends, using multi-tracking to multiply the voices.

Commercial recordings of selections from his *Morse* music have proved very successful, the first becoming a platinum disc.

He has made one anonymous appearance on screen. In the opening sequence of *Masonic Mysteries*, he is disguised in an outsized bird's head as *The Magic Flute*'s Papageno.

One-man orchestra – the Pheloung phenomenon.

PHILLIPSON, DONALD

The headmaster of the ROGER BACON COMPREHENSIVE SCHOOL is interviewed and appointed in *Last Seen Wearing*: Prologue – after which he is 'naughty' with Valerie Taylor and sets in train the puzzling sequence of events investigated by Morse and Lewis two years later.

Although Phillipson comes close to public disgrace, he is not a murderer and Morse elects not to let him be ruined. In *Service of All the Dead*: 17 Phillipson is still in his post when Morse consults him about the music teacher on his staff, Paul Morris. And, of course, he is 'only too pleased to be of help', plying Morse with sherry and letting him consult the records with no questions asked. His namesake, the headmaster in the film version of *Last Seen Wearing*, is in a very different position and does not get off so lightly.

PHOBIAS, MORSE'S

> Morse, as Lewis knew only too well, was a man prepared to take the most prodigious leaps into the dark. (*Service of All the Dead*: 22)

Not literally, however, for a fear of the dark – which he has had since childhood – is one of Morse's phobias, of which he has a whole sackful. He is afraid of heights (hypsophobia) and of flying (aerophobia), of spiders (arachnophobia) and – notoriously – of corpses (necrophobia).

But there is an even more personal phobia in Morse's psyche, and it is perhaps the most primitive fear of all: the fear of *revealing his own name*. This is almost an occult preoccupation – as if the revelation will give others some power over him which he will be unable to counter. He begins to overcome this debilitating problem only in *Death is Now My Neighbour*: Envoi, when he at last writes a card to Lewis signing himself 'Endeavour'.

PITT-RIVERS MUSEUM, THE

This collection of ethnological artefacts and remains, assembled by General Pitt-Rivers, was gifted to the university in 1884 and is attached to the University Museum in South Parks Road. The weapon used to kill Edward Brooks was part of its collection – a Barotse tribal ceremonial knife from Zambia, once owned by Zeta the Third, Paramount Chief (*The Daughters of Cain*: 38).

The murder weapon as museum piece – The Daughters of Cain.

POLICE PROCEDURE(S)

DAWSON: You'll get there, Morse. You're a good detective.
MORSE: But a bad policeman?
DAWSON: I think so, yes. The law is our only weapon, Morse. Good policemen have no wish to see it weakened.
MORSE: I work with what's laid down.
DAWSON: Neutral? You're hardly that, Morse. Your views are known. (*Second Time Around*)

Morse may claim to 'work with what's laid down' but he does not care much about proper procedure, and nor does Colin Dexter. Morse – like Dexter – is interested first in the puzzle and second in justice. He will do anything in his power, however unorthodox, to crack the first and bring about the second – whether it is breaking and entering (*The Daughters of Cain, Death is Now My Neighbour*), forging letters (*Last Seen Wearing*), sending pseudo-Victorian verses packed with clues to *The Times* (*The Way Through the Woods*) searching without warrant (*Driven to Distraction*), investigating another officer's case (*Last Seen Wearing, Service of All the Dead, Masonic Mysteries, The Way Through the Woods*) or posing improbably as an expert on the breeding and raising of cattle (*Promised Land*).

Morse hates routine, although when he wants to be he is 'an extremely competent administrator' (*The Riddle of the Third Mile*: 10) and, if the mood is on him, capable of a ferocious work rate. At other times his procedures when conducting an inquiry can be anarchic and lackadaisical. He constructs chimerical theories, relying on hunches and random association – more like a poet than a policeman, and usually with several glasses of real ale inside him.

This leads to all sorts of problems: 'Often in the past Morse had similarly been six or so furlongs ahead of the field only later to find himself running on the wrong racecourse' (*The Way Through the Woods*: 46).

The test of a theory for Morse is the prickling around the shoulders and the hair rising around the nape of his neck. If he feels those symptoms, he always knows he is on to something.

POLITICS

'I've never heard so many lies – it's like sitting through an election campaign,' says Morse in *Second Time Around* after interrogating a suspect. He is a cynic about politics, though he does have broadly liberal beliefs. However, at times he will embrace both quasi-socialist and frankly reactionary political opinions. In *The Jewel That Was Ours*: 25 we find Morse arguing for subsidized public transport, particularly the railways, on which, despite his love for his CAR, he enjoys travelling. His interest in PORNOGRAPHY would make him strongly against any wide-ranging censorship in this area and he is also definitely against capital punishment, as we learn in *Second Time Around*. As a delegate of the Police Federation, he had travelled to Blackpool in the late 1960s to speak against hanging in a conference debate – 'my first public speech . . . we lost'.

He balances this liberalism by swinging over to reaction on the question of drugs – 'all drugs are evil' (*Cherubim and Seraphim*) – and adopting a generally scornful view of MODERN LIFE and progressive causes, which makes him appear rather more conservative than he really is.

In any event, Morse is unlikely to support any party in a formal sense, as he suffers too much from social pessimism. Again, from *Cherubim and Seraphim*:

> 'What sort of a life do we offer our young people, Lewis? School. If you're lucky, college. Then marriage. A "starter home", then children. A two-bedroom semi. If you do well you've just about got four bedrooms when your kids leave to buy "starter homes" of their own . . . This British home-owning democracy we're so proud of – it's really a form of slavery. Man was born free, but everywhere he's in the property chain.'

PORNOGRAPHY

Pornography usually gets into a Morse novel one way or another and, to a lesser extent, features in the TV film series: porn photography as private hobby in *The Ghost in the Machine*, *Who Killed Harry Field?* and *The Way Through the Woods*; addiction to porn in *Last Bus to Woodstock*, *The Jewel That Was Ours*, *The Way Through the Woods* and 'As Good as Gold'. In *The Silent World of Nicholas Quinn*, the entire staff of the examinations syndicate appears to have been to see the film *The Nymphomaniac* at the time of the murder. In *The Riddle of the Third Mile*: 34 Morse picks up a book which a nightclub bouncer is reading because the title interests him – *Know Your Köchel Numbers* – and finds beneath the cover 'a load of the lewdest pornography I've ever seen. I've, er, got it with me, if you'd like to borrow it, Lewis.'

Morse has a pronounced curiosity about pornography and browses enthusiastically through the copies of 'top-shelf' magazines that he regularly finds while searching suspicious premises. In *The Wench is Dead*, Lewis, who knows his boss so well, brings him a titillating novel in hospital entitled *The Blue Ticket*. Morse comments, 'I hope you don't read this kind of rubbish, Lewis', but his own surreptitious efforts to read the book on the ward become one of the recurring comic motifs of the story. In *Death is Now My Neighbour*, when burgling Geoff Owens's house with his housebreaker acquaintance, J.J., in search of evidence, he is tempted to purloin a book, *Topless in Torremolinos*, and slips it into his pocket. Then, noticing that J.J. has stolen a clock, he sternly reproves him before guiltily replacing the book where he found it.

PRISON

Morse supports the prison system more or less in its existing form, partly because of a lurking scepticism about facile liberalism, and partly because he is serenely confident about his ability to catch real villains who are thoroughly deserving of a rigorous, old-fashioned punishment.

In *Masonic Mysteries* Morse prides himself on never having put away anyone who didn't deserve it, although in *Second Time Around* and *Absolute Conviction* he has to deal with the fall-out from miscarriages of justice for which his colleagues had been responsible. In the second of these films he is attracted to Hilary Stevens (Diana Quick), the liberal governor of Farnleigh experimental prison, where a prisoner has been murdered. Morse is at first scornful of Farnleigh, calling it a 'country club' and remarking mysteriously, 'knock on the front door and you've got the Chief Constable on your back'. But Governor Hilary Stevens's efforts in running a liberal prison nevertheless interest him. This is perhaps not least because Governor Hilary Stevens interests him, but Morse is also prompted by the plight of the wrongly convicted Charlie Bennett. In the end, as Stevens's career hangs in the balance, he is anxious to know she won't give up the struggle to put her ideas into practice.

Morse's proud boast that he has never had an innocent man jailed is put to the test and found wanting in *Promised Land*. Here the consequences of the unjust conviction of Peter Matthews, arrested by Morse in Oxford after a bank raid and now dead from AIDS in prison, send him and Lewis to the other side of the world, where Morse is almost killed into the bargain.

See also POLITICS.

PRODUCERS OF THE MORSE FILMS

Executive Producer for all the *Morse* films, Ted Childs, can take credit for launching Dexter's novels on TELEVISION. Formerly producer of John THAW's series *The Sweeney*, Childs was Controller of Drama at Central Television in the late 1980s when he needed a police drama set within the Midland company's transmission area. Morse's Oxford fitted the bill perfectly.

The first producer of *Morse* on television, and the man to whom all involved in the series pay tribute as its visionary force, was Kenny McBain. McBain, who had previously produced the comedy-thriller series *Boon* for Central Television and worked on *Auf Wiedersehen, Pet*, where he met Kevin Whately, brought in the high-quality writers and directors and conceived the then revolutionary idea for a series of two-hour episodes. After working on two series, McBain left to develop *Sharpe* and then fell ill with Hodgkin's disease. He died in April 1989.

Chris Burt.

Culture Clash: Morse thinks Australia is a cultural desert while Australians think he's a teetotaller.

In *Driven to Distraction*, Anthony Minghella wrote a melancholy little speech for Morse: 'Sad, isn't it – how all the domestic things become ridiculous when someone dies . . . I had a friend who died, he'd been ill for ages and he was worried that his car battery would go flat. Every Friday I used to go round, drive the car round the block for twenty minutes, to keep it . . . And then he died. He hadn't driven the car in a year.' This friend was really Minghella's – Kenny McBain.

Chris Burt, who took over in series three, later produced both series seven and the three single films. He had previously worked with John Thaw on *The Sweeney*. Series four and five were produced by David Lascelles and series six by Deirdre Keir.

PROMISED LAND (TV film only)

Thames Valley's prize supergrass Kenny Stone and his family have been provided with a new life in Australia. But at the funeral of one of the men convicted on his evidence, dead from prison-contracted AIDS, it occurs to STRANGE and Morse to wonder if Stone told all about the Abingdon bank raid ten years back. Now that a campaign has started to discredit the original police evidence, Morse and Lewis are sent out to reinterview him in the remote New South Wales township where he has settled. It turns out, however, that the Thames Valley CID are not the only ones trying to contact the former villain, and the 'routine' inquiry becomes an ordeal of suspense as Stone disappears, his mother-in-law is attacked and dies, and his daughter is kidnapped. Morse is clearly not the only one in pursuit of Stone.

Morse is instinctively at odds with the aggressive earthiness of Australian culture and his feelings are characteristically expressed. 'They don't spell Australian beer with four XXXX's out of ignorance,' he says, ordering an orange juice in a bar while Lewis has Lite beer. 'They mean what they say. And Lite beer is an invention of the Prince of Darkness.'

Meanwhile, the local police discover that Morse, who poses at first as a Ministry of Agriculture official and then as a private eye, has been lying to them. Relations deteriorate, with Morse treating the local coppers as idiots, while they regard him sourly as an arrogant, interfering and, what's worse, so they think, teetotal pom who hasn't heard about the end of the empire. The convention so natural in Oxford, whereby Lewis always defers to Morse, calling him 'sir' and submitting meekly to his brusque commands, is clearly out of place in this atmosphere showing the formality and artifice of the relationship with a new clarity.

The possibility that the Abingdon bank raid had ended in a miscarriage of justice – and an unpleasant prison death – increasingly haunts Morse, who feels his journey into this hostile, unfamiliar environment is a kind of punishment: 'I've always prided myself I've never sent anyone to prison who didn't belong there.' But now he has even worse events to blame himself for – three deaths and an unresolved kidnapping. In an uncharacteristically humble confession, while arguing why he should offer himself to the kidnapper as a substitute for Stone's daughter, he tells Lewis, 'Ron Pigot and I started in the force together and when he was shot in the [Abingdon] raid I wanted revenge. It's a powerful emotion. It blinds you. I let myself be blinded. I have to make amends.'

First transmission 27 March 1991
Writer Julian Mitchell
Director John Madden
Cast includes Rhondda Findleton, John Jarratt

PSYCHOLOGY

One of Morse's favourite psychological maxims, adapted from Lord Byron, is mentioned in *Greeks Bearing Gifts*: 'Watch the mouth. It gives away what the eye tries to hide.' At times Morse shows a policeman's instinctive sense of psychology. He employs an effective technique of psychological harassment to put pressure on Jeremy Boynton in *Driven to Distraction* – to no purpose, as it happens – and he skilfully breaks down the resistance of the bland PHILLIPSON in the film version of *Last Seen Wearing*. In *Deceived by Flight* he senses that Anthony Donn has a problem, something he wants to discuss with Morse.

But Morse is no Dr Fitzgerald from *Cracker* and would scoff at psychological profiling, probably wisely, since his own less than perfect psychological understanding frequently puts him at a loss. In *The Death of the Self* he fails completely to see why Russell Clarke's encounter group should have any success; in *Cherubim and Seraphim* he struggles in vain to comprehend the mind of a contemporary teenager and he fatally fails to pick up the undercurrent of rage against the Japanese nation in *The Settling of the Sun*.

PUBLIC HOUSE(S)

Morse has an old-fashioned, perhaps romantic but absolutely right attitude to pubs. They are, or should be, places in which to meet, drink cask-conditioned beer and talk – or to think by oneself, as Morse often does. Loud music, and most certainly muzak, are fatal impediments to these objectives.

Some of Morse's favourite watering holes in Oxford are the TURF TAVERN, close to New College; the Mitre on the High Street; the RANDOLPH HOTEL (*Service of All the Dead*, *The Jewel That Was Ours*); the EAGLE AND CHILD; the Bulldog, ST ALDATES; the BEAR INN; the Cherwell, Water Eaton Road; the King's Arms, Banbury Road ('Neighbourhood Watch', *The Daughters of Cain*); the 'Printer's Devil' (i.e. the Bookbinder's Arms), and the Anchor, both in JERICHO; the Marsh Harrier, Cowley Road, Cowley (*The Daughters of Cain*); the King's Arms, Parks Road (*Death is Now My Neighbour*); and the White Horse near BLACKWELL'S BOOKSHOP. Outside Oxford, there are prominent mentions for the Bull and Swan, KIDLINGTON; the 'Black Prince' (loosely based on the Bear Inn), WOODSTOCK; the Boat Inn at Thrupp; the Trout at Godstow; the White Hart at Wytham (*The Way Through the Woods*) and the 'Peep of Dawn' in Reading (*The Secret of Annexe 3*).

To Morse, the pub is an extension of the office. Here, in Masonic Mysteries, *he and Lewis catch up on the paperwork in the Fighting Cocks.*

· R ·

RADCLIFFE INFIRMARY AND THE JOHN RADCLIFFE HOSPITAL (JR2)

These are two distinct hospitals. In *Death is Now My Neighbour*, suddenly struck with a new HEALTH crisis, Morse is admitted to the Radcliffe Infirmary, just north of St Giles's at the bottom of the Woodstock Road. This hospital – Oxford's historic (1770) teaching hospital – stands next to the Radcliffe Observatory which, no doubt to Morse's great delight, is modelled on the rather smaller Tower of Winds in Athens, where the first weathercock stood. Staff Nurse Widdowson in *Last Bus to Woodstock* works at the Infirmary, and it is also to the casualty department here that Morse takes his injured foot after falling through a ladder.

In *The Wench is Dead*, on the other hand, Morse is confined in the modern JR2 in HEADINGTON. Of this, Dexter had already written:

> Few of the buildings erected in Oxford since the end of the Second World War have
> met with approval from either Town or Gown . . . but it is generally agreed that the
> John Radcliffe Hospital on Headington Hill is one of the least offensive examples of
> modern design . . . (*The Silent World of Nicholas Quinn*: 10)

In *The Wench is Dead* Morse certainly receives excellent care there. The JR2 is also in the film of *Last Bus to Woodstock*, where the nurses work under the beady eye of a time-and-motion study, and it is in the JR2 car park that we see Julia Stevens and Brenda Brooks, in the first scene of *The Daughters of Cain*, reacting to the news that Julia has an inoperable brain tumour.

The Radcliffe Infirmary.

RADIO

Morse is chronologically and temperamentally pre-television but he likes the radio, listening to THE ARCHERS devotedly and showing more than once an interest in *Desert Island Discs*. For MUSIC he seems equally enthusiastic about BBC Radio Three and the commercial station Classic FM.

Morse has also been heard on BBC Radio Four. One story, 'The Burglar', has been read and four novels dramatized – *Last Bus to Woodstock* (1985), *The Wench is Dead* (1992), *Last Seen Wearing* (1994) and *The Silent World of Nicholas Quinn* (1997). In the dramatizations, Morse is played by John Shrapnel and Lewis by Robert Glenister.

When on 1 February 1998 Colin Dexter was invited to choose his own *Desert Island Discs*, the following were his eight selections:

1. 'In Paradisum' from *Requiem* by Gabriel Fauré, Westminster Cathedral Choir with the City of London Symphonium, conducted by David Hill.
2. *Abide with Me*, performed by Dame Clara Butt.
3. Étude No. 5, op. 25 by Frédéric Chopin, played by Vladimir Ashkenazy.
4. Clarinet Concerto in A major K. 622 by Mozart. Jack Brymer with the BBC Symphony Orchestra, conducted by Sir Malcolm Sargent.
5. 'The Long and Winding Road' from *Let It Be* by The Beatles.
6. Gerard Hoffnung live from the OXFORD UNION SOCIETY: 'The Bricklayer'.
7. 'On Going to Sleep' *Four Last Songs* no. 3 by Richard Strauss, sung by Lisa della Casa.
8. Extract from the finale of *Götterdämmerung* by Richard WAGNER, Orchestra of La Scala, Milan, conducted by Wilhelm Furtwängler and with Kirsten Flagstad as Brünnhilde.

Dexter's chosen book was the collected poetry and classical papers of A. E. HOUSMAN. His one permitted 'luxury' was a pair of nail scissors.

The Randolph Hotel.

RANDOLPH HOTEL

Dating from 1864 and extended in 1952, this is Oxford's most famous hotel, a splendidly Gothic building on the corner of Beaumont Street and Magdalen Street. Although its character is in stark contrast to his favourite PUBLIC HOUSES, Morse considers that 'they serve a decent pint' and is a regular patron of the bar. The hotel features prominently in *Service of All the Dead*, *The Jewel That Was Ours*, *The Wolvercote Tongue*, 'Last Call' and *Second Time Around*.

See also HARDEN, ROY.

RELIGION

Morse's mother was a Quaker but he himself had shed his 'early ebullient faith'. Apart from a sincere (if not always adhered to) belief in the spiritual value of hard work, he was largely unscathed by Christianity, so that when in *Fat Chance* he is asked if he believes in God, Morse can only reply 'sometimes when I'm listening to music . . .' and leaves the rest of the thought trailing away into imprecision. The truth is that Morse thinks 'the teachings of the church so much gobbledegook' (*Service of All the Dead*: 34) and 'his philosophy of life amounted to little more than a heap of confused impressions, akin to those of a bewildered young boy at a conjuring show' (6).

Yet Morse 'retains a sort of residual religiosity' which, at times, he wishes would blossom into something more tangible:

> LEWIS: What do you think . . . about God and that? Do you think there's a God?
> MORSE: (*sighs*) I think . . . there are times when I wish to God there was one. A just god. A god dispensing justice. I'd like to believe in that. (*Promised Land*)

RETIREMENT

Morse and STRANGE discuss this in *The Daughters of Cain*: 1. Strange is thinking of 'jacking in the job' in a year or two's time – under pressure from Mrs Strange more than anything. Morse admits he too has been thinking of retirement, but neither man will really engage with the task of filling in the necessary forms, claiming it gives them a headache. However, it is not the forms themselves but the thought of months and years of unstructured idleness ahead that brings them pain.

RIDDLE OF THE THIRD MILE, THE (novel, 1983)

'Aren't you making it all a bit too complicated?' asks Lewis in Chapter 19, once again playing the anvil on which his chief can hammer out some of his more twisted ideas. But nothing can be too complicated for Morse, who 'always had the greatest faith in the policy of mouthing the most improbable notions, in the sure certainty that by the law of averages some of them stood a chance of being nearer to the truth than others'.

The story begins when a dismembered and headless corpse turns up in the OXFORD CANAL and it is not until the very last pages that the identity of the victim is known. This is the start of the long vacation and the college dons have headed off to all points of the compass. Morse has early indications that the dead man may be his own old classics tutor, Browne-Smith, murdered by a hated college rival, Westerby. There again, the body may be Westerby, murdered by Browne-Smith. Or the corpse (or the murderer) may be one of a pair of twins called Gilbert, both harbouring a grudge against Browne-Smith which dates back to the Second World War.

Means, opportunity, motive – there are too many players in this drama who have all three of the essential qualifications for murderer and Morse finds out much in the course of his unusually energetic inquiries, but chiefly about the extent of his own ignorance:

> Morse was acutely conscious of the truth of the proposition that the wider the circle of knowledge the greater the circumference of ignorance. He was like some tree-feller in the midst of the deepest forest who has effected a clearing large enough for his immediate purposes; but one, too, who sees around him the widening rim of undiscovered darkness wherein the wickedness of other men would never be wholly revealed. (35)

By the time the Chief Inspector has cleared the area of forest in which all the secrets are hidden, he has had some interesting experiences in the sex district of Soho, enjoyed a tantalizing flirtation with a high-class tart and suffered a savage toothache. He solves the mystery with the aid of the Bible when, lying alone in bed in a seedy London hotel, a scriptural tag springs to his mind. Associated as it is with the forgiveness of enemies – one of the case's main themes – he looks it up courtesy of the Gideon Society: 'And whosoever shall compel thee to go a mile, go with him twain (Matthew 5.41).' He lets the associations play over his mind and then (30)

> it was with the forty-watt bulb shedding its feeble light over the Gideon Bible that Morse smiled in unspeakable joy, like one who has travelled on a longer journey still – that third and final mile . . .
>   *At last he knew the truth.*

It is an abstruse and, for Morse, private key to the mystery, enabling him to make one of those legendary leaps of associative intuition. But, this aside, it is one Morse mystery where all the required information is available for the reader to solve the case well before Dexter finally reveals the truth.

See also: LAST ENEMY, THE.

RIVERS

Oxford lies between and across two rivers, the Isis (i.e. the Thames or *Thamesis* in Latin) and the Cherwell, a tributary which joins the Thames just south of CHRIST CHURCH Meadow. In *The Daughters of Cain*: 55 the body of the corrupt ex-college scout Ted Brooks is found beside the boathouse at the Riverside Centre towards Iffley, a quarter of a mile south of the convergence of the two streams. In *The Jewel That Was Ours* the body of Dr Theodore Kemp is recovered at PARSON'S PLEASURE on the Cherwell, although in *The Wolvercote Tongue* he is found in the Isis at WOLVERCOTE.

ROGER BACON COMPREHENSIVE SCHOOL, KIDLINGTON

This school (Headmaster D. PHILLIPSON), a more or less typical representative of secondary EDUCATION in Britain, appears in the novel *Last Seen Wearing* (though not the film, where it becomes an expensive private girls' school) and *Service of All the Dead*.

ROMANCE

Morse is attractive to women and he is also attracted *to* them. This is a key element in most of the novels and films. But in line with his overall 1950s profile, romance is a curiously old-fashioned business – *Brief Encounter* rather than *Basic Instinct*, Vera Lynn rather than the Rolling Stones. This does not just apply to Morse's own amours. Sue and her fiancé David in *Last Bus to Woodstock* are a couple out of a Leatherhead tearoom *circa*

The Isis from Folly Bridge, c. 1900.

The River Cherwell above the University Parks, near Lady Margaret Hall, c. 1895.

1952 and the adulterous shenanigans at the Haworth Hotel in *The Secret of Annexe 3* seem to lag well behind the sexual revolution.

Morse's own romantic life is always overshadowed by nostalgic memories of past girl-friends. In *The Silent World of Nicholas Quinn*: 14, 'It all came back to him in a rushing stream of recollection. He'd been an undergraduate then and he'd invited the flighty little nurse back to his digs in Iffley Road . . .' In *The Riddle of the Third Mile*: 29 Morse is aflutter at the thought he may be about to see Wendy Spencer again, 'the woman whom he'd worshipped all those years ago . . . It couldn't be the same woman and yet ye gods – if gods ye be – please make it her!'

Morse's imagination, and its favourite literary food, is in tune with all this overall sense of nostalgia and amorous loss. Hardy and HOUSMAN predominate and 'the saddest line of poetry he had ever read' (*Last Bus to Woodstock*: 18) is from Hardy's 'Thoughts of Phena': 'Not a line of her writing have I, not a thread of her hair.'

In the films the spirit of all this is faithfully adhered to. Time and again Morse is drawn to inappropriate women. Indeed, in no less than a third of the episodes (*The Daughters of Cain*, *The Day of the Devil*, *Deadly Slumber*, *Dead on Time*, *Deceived by Flight*, *Happy Families*, *Last Bus to Woodstock*, *Masonic Mysteries*, *Service of All the Dead* and *The Settling of the Sun*) he falls for women who are either murderers or accessories to murder. The

Brief Encounter: *a concept with which Morse is all-too familiar.*

most traumatic of these is *Dead on Time*, in which Morse enacts the ordeal of finding, and once again losing, his long-lost love. Morse's yearnings are frequently mocked, especially when (as in the case of Drs RUSSELL and HOBSON and Detective Sergeant Maitland in *Driven to Distraction*) they seem to be tending in the direction of an 'office romance'. But in *Dead on Time*, when he simultaneously investigates the murder of Susan Fallon's husband and tries to win back her love, his predicament is treated sympathetically and without irony. The result is genuinely moving.

RUSSELL, DR GRAYLING

Dr Russell (Amanda Hillwood), the PATHOLOGIST who replaces Max de BRYN, enters the scene in the third television series in *The Ghost in the Machine*. Morse struggles to accept a woman as a pathologist ('You shouldn't let a woman look at battered heads like that'), but having got over that hurdle he grows to like her, particularly because both have eccentric first names. Typically, while he still won't reveal his own, in *The Last Enemy* Dr Russell is prepared to tell him about hers.

> RUSSELL: Blame my father. I was his seventh daughter and he was a keen fisherman and desperate for a name. He decided to call me after whatever he pulled out of the river.
> MORSE: Lucky it wasn't a chub, then.

Amanda Hillwood as Dr Grayling Russell in The Secret of Bay 5B.

In the same film Lewis too finds common ground, for Dr Russell trained at Newcastle General Hospital.

> LEWIS: You'd have made a smashing GP. What made you prefer dead bodies?
> RUSSELL: You have the same challenge of diagnosis but without the responsibility of prescription.

Dr Russell disappears from the world of Morse – presumably thanks to a promotion elsewhere – after *The Secret of Bay 5B*. This is just at the point when the relationship is beginning to show promise after they go together to a performance of *Parsifal*.

· S ·

ST ALDATE'S

The street in central Oxford which runs south from Carfax and past CHRIST CHURCH. It is also the address of the headquarters of Oxford City Police, where Morse settles cuckoo-like to pursue his unofficial inquiries in *Service of All the Dead*. In *The Sins of the Fathers* the corrupt solicitor Alfred Nelson has his office in this street and is murdered there.

ST CROSS CHURCH, HOLYWELL

Standing on St Cross Road close to the Magdalen deer park, this church was the important location for filming *Service of All the Dead*.

ST FRIDESWIDE'S CHURCH

This fictional church, in which multiple violent deaths occur in *Service of All the Dead* (it is called St Oswald's in the film) is perhaps based on a mixture of St Michael-by-the-North-Gate on Cornmarket (with its Saxon tower, Oxford's oldest building) and St Mary Magdalen ('St Mary Mags') on Magdalen Street, a mixture of medieval and Gothic-revival architecture. St Frideswide, who died *circa* 735, was 'a daughter of the King of Mercia who fled to Oxford to preserve her virginity from an importunate prince' (*Greeks Bearing Gifts*) becoming an anchorite at Binsey, close to Oxford. She is the patron of Oxford and the remains of a large medieval abbey of St Fridewide's were incorporated into the cathedral.

The murder site of Service of All the Dead *is in reality St Cross Church, Holywell.*

'I don't like this kind of church,' Morse tells Lewis in the film *Service of All the Dead*. This is because St Frideswide's – like St Mary Mags – is traditional and High Church, with candles, incense and much talk of Mass and the sacraments. All this 'gobbledegook' makes Morse, with no RELIGION of his own, twitch in discomfort.

ST SAVIOUR'S COLLEGE

The fictional college in *Fat Chance* where the battle for the chaplaincy between traditionalists and feminists is fought out.

SCRIPTWRITERS

The first writer recruited to Morse – for *The Dead of Jericho* – was Anthony Minghella, who has since won multiple Oscars for the feature film, which he wrote and directed, *The English Patient*. He scripted two further *Morse* films, *Deceived by Flight* and *Driven to Distraction*. By far the most prolific writer in the series has been the playwright Julian Mitchell (nine films), whom the curious can see and hear performing as a publican in *Cherubim and Seraphim*. Just two other individuals have written more than one episode. Daniel Boyle, who has written six films, is not to be confused with Danny Boyle, director of *Masonic Mysteries* and *Cherubim and Seraphim* (and also of the successful feature films, *Shallow Grave* and *Trainspotting*. Alma Cullen, credited with four films, is the only woman to have written a *Morse*.

Storylines for the first three series were based either on the Morse novels or on detailed plot outlines commissioned from Colin Dexter (and credited as 'an idea by Colin Dexter'). Thereafter, except for adaptations of three further novels scriptwriters were responsible for the storyline, in consultation with Morse's creator.

SECOND TIME AROUND (TV film only)

A retired ace detective, Charlie Hillian, is murdered just as he finishes his memoirs – and one chapter of the manuscript is found to be missing.

> MORSE: What was the chapter about?
> MAJORS: It was about a tragedy, Inspector. As dark as any. It was seventeen, eighteen years ago. The murder of a child. She was, I believe, eight years old. Her name was –
> MORSE: Mary Lapsley.
> MAJORS: The very same, Inspector. You were involved?

Yes, Morse *was* involved. It had been he who found the child's body, though this was Hillian's investigation, and he never discovered the killer's identity. Dogged by accusations of professional jealousy from Hillian's old colleague Dawson (Kenneth Colley) and – worse – from Lewis, both of whom say he is wrong, Morse again ploughs a lone furrow in the inquiry, until he turns up the true connection between the murders of Hillian and Mary Lapsley. At one stroke, he has solved two completely dissimilar murders committed eighteen years apart.

This is only one of two Morse cases involving the killing of a child. In the other, *Service of All the Dead*, Paul Morris's death is as much as anything a by-product of the murderer's general wickedness. Here horror and the passions the killing of Mary Lapsley arouses are central to the case. Worked like an almost invisible thread into the fabric of the script is the debate within the police force about capital punishment – a motion to which both Morse and Dawson had spoken at a Police Federation conference more than twenty years before. It is an example of the subtle and skilful way the *Morse* films have often dealt with complex public issues.

First transmission 20 February 1991
Writer Daniel Boyle
Director Adrian Shergold
Cast includes Adie Allen, Ann Bell, Kenneth Colley, Oliver Ford Davies, Christopher Ecclestone, Pat Heywood

SECRET OF ANNEXE 3, THE (novel, 1986)

'We've been on a lot of cases together Lewis – with lots of people involved; but I don't reckon the motives are ever all that different – love, hate, jealousy, revenge.'
(*The Secret of Annexe 3*: 36)

Morse's investigation of the death of a man in fancy dress at an Oxford hotel once again explores the eternal verities of murder. Hotels are, of course, ideal territory for the who-dunnit. A disparate group of people is brought together under a single roof where, away from their home routines, they can be relied upon to loosen the conventions and constraints which normally bind them. The masks they wear slip and their true destiny emerges, whether as bullies, swindlers, fornicators, blackmailers, murderers or – it being mandatory that there is at least one of these – corpses.

The tragic outcome of the New Year's Eve weekend at the Haworth Hotel, an establishment based on the OLD PARSONAGE HOTEL, present Morse with all the ingredients of a highly enjoyable investigation. The guests were in impenetrable fancy dress; several had not checked in under their true identities; juicy red herrings occupied the adjacent rooms; and heavy snowfall during the night enabled inferences to be made from the footprint evidence.

Dexter is at his teasing best here as he lays out selective details of all the lives caught up in these events – just enough to keep you guessing, never enough (until the end) to settle the issue. Meanwhile, Morse fits the pieces of the puzzle into one variant solution after another, each as elegant as its predecessor (his solutions are never more elegant than when they are wrong) and is hardly even put off his stride by the love letter he receives from one of the female witnesses.

As a theorist Morse usually has plenty to say about his ideas and methods. One remark made to Lewis in Chapter 17 of this novel, at the height of their bafflement, reveals his lurking belief that police work frequently produces strange distortions in one's common perception of normality: 'Perhaps – the thought suddenly struck him – it was the masks that were the reality, and the faces beneath them that were the pretence.' Typically, this inspirational paradox provides Morse with a new direction and, eventually, a solution to the crime.

SECRET OF BAY 5B, THE (TV film only)

Morse is dancing the quickstep with Dr Grayling RUSSELL at a ball in the TOWN HALL when Lewis arrives to summon them both to look at a corpse at the WESTGATE CAR PARK, a few hundred yards away. The investigation into the strangling of architect Michael Gifford in his car throws up the usual confusion of suspects, including the manager of an insurance company, an alcoholic forester at WYTHAM WOODS and a thwarted junior architect at Gifford's practice with a habit of dipping his fingers into the till. For once, Morse goes methodically about his task, working his way through the possibilities until he isolates the guilty person.

The romance with Dr Russell that had been slowly evolving throughout the third series of television films still looks promising in this, the last episode. It ends with Morse and the attractive pathologist planning their date, which will include a performance of Wagner's *Parsifal*. But perhaps, after all, the date went badly, for this would turn out to be the last episode to feature Dr Grayling Russell as Morse's pathologist.

First transmission 25 January 1989
Writer Alma Cullen, based on an idea by Colin Dexter
Director Jim Goddard
Cast includes Marion Bailey, Philip McGough, Mel Martin, Andrew Wilde

'You can quick-step, Morse!' Morse's dance with Dr Russell is interrupted when they are both called to a nearby murder.

SERVICE OF ALL THE DEAD (novel, 1979)

Morse, going out of his mind with boredom during a period of spring leave, finds himself pondering a bizarre six-month-old incident which had happened in Oxford while he was 'away on an eight-week secondment in West AFRICA'. Of two deaths at the parish church of ST FRIDESWIDE'S on the Cornmarket, one was undoubtedly murder, apparently in the middle of a church service, using poisoned Holy Communion wine and a paper knife in the form of a crucifix. The second death, that of the vicar, was deemed to be suicide out of remorse for the murder he had committed. Such, at least, were the findings of Morse's old adversary within the force, Chief Inspector BELL. Naturally enough, as he casually ponders the case, Morse cannot agree.

He immediately starts building complicated hypotheses on the foundations of the established facts, drawn further into the subject by the attraction he feels for Ruth Rawlinson, the thirty-something parish stalwart who cleans the church. The circle of suspects in the case were as closely involved in each other's lives as with the incense-laden High Church rituals preferred by the vicar. The organist, a music teacher at the ROGER BACON COMPREHENSIVE SCHOOL, was having an affair with the wife of the gambling-addict church warden, who was himself having an affair with Morse's friend Ruth. The homosexual vicar was being blackmailed and finally there was the old tramp who had lately been hanging around and even occasionally attended Mass.

Then Morse discovers another body and it is clear that Bell's closure of the case had been premature. And the body count rises – at five, this is as high as they come in *Morse*, and none by natural causes. With the church tower a key location for several of the deaths, one of Morse's worst PHOBIAS, his vertigo, puts him as severely to the test as ever James Stewart was challenged in the film by Alfred Hitchcock.

Dexter's chapters are appropriately divided into four sections: two *Books of Chronicles*, a *Book of Revelations* and a *Book of Ruth*. One revelation we never hear, however, is what Morse was up to in West Africa.

SERVICE OF ALL THE DEAD (TV film)

The Lawson brothers become the Pawlen brothers and ST FRIDESWIDE'S CHURCH becomes St Oswald's, yet this is one of the most faithful screen adaptations of a Morse novel. At the same time, Peter Hammond's direction is especially filmic, always seeking out unusual shots and angles, constantly working with reflections and shadows to exploit the symmetries and variations of Dexter's and screenwriter Mitchell's themes.

Those themes centre on the different ways in which human unhappiness is borne or escaped from: through sexual passion in the case of the church organist Paul Morris; through drink, like Morse himself and the tramp 'Swanpole'; through religion or, like Harry Josephs, gambling ('the Church and the Turf are old friends, you know,' says one

'I hate this kind of Church.' But sometimes religious observance is part of the job for Morse and Lewis.

character); and finally, when all these fail and desperation takes hold, in violence and murder.

There are intriguing outside references too, seeded here like cryptic clues. At one point Samuel Beckett's tramps in *Waiting for Godot* supply Morse with a parallel to his own inquiries. At another, with Morse chasing the murderer up the spiral stairs of St Oswald's tower, we see a parody of the climactic scene in Hitchcock's *Vertigo*.

First transmission 20 January 1987
Writer Julian Mitchell
Director Peter Hammond
Cast includes Michael Hordern, Angela Morant, John Normington

SETTLING OF THE SUN, THE (TV film only)

Based on Colin Dexter's own story, this is morally one of the grimmest of all the *Morse* films. Like *The Jewel That Was Ours*, it concerns a group of foreigners new to Oxford, although this time they are not tourists but students attending a summer school at LONS-DALE COLLEGE. On the first evening, one of them – a young Japanese named Yukio Li – is found dead, crucified to the floor of his room in an apparently ritualized killing. But Morse, lovesick for the tense and neurotic course organizer Dr Jane Robson only slowly

Sir Wilfrid Mulryne at High Table and in full flow. But in another part of the college a murder has been committed.

brings his incisive mind to bear on the case. Yet again, he is wasting his time.

> JANE: I never had any feelings for you.
> MORSE: That became obvious . . .

It presents him with a tangle of motives – war crimes, jealousy, drugs – but memories of the war in the Far East loom particularly large. The college Master Sir Wilfrid Mulryne (Robert Stephens at his best) is a cynical, disappointed man whose son has died from drugs. But does Mulryne harbour an equally deep hatred of Japan, after his experiences interrogating prisoners during the war? Others undoubtedly do have bitter memories of the war with Japan. One is Dr Robson herself, whose late father was tortured by the Japanese; another is the college's domestic bursar, Mrs Warbut (skilfully played by Avis Bunnage), who rarely wastes an opportunity to air her views. Outside the college chapel is a memorial tablet to overseas members of the college who lost their lives in the war, irrespective of what country they fought for. Mrs Warbut sees Morse reading it.

> MORSE: Fair enough, I suppose.
> MRS WARBUT: Is it? I don't think so.
> MORSE: (*to himself*) No, you probably wouldn't.

Then drugs enter the equation, with traces of heroin found in a package left in the summer-school bus and the information that Yukio Li was a drugs dealer. And with one of the summer-school students exposed as 'a phoney', Morse is off on another line of inquiry, until he realizes that he has been set up from the start, by the one person involved whom he hoped would be his friend.

First transmission 15 March 1988
Writer Charles Wood, based on an idea by Colin Dexter
Director Peter Hammond
Cast includes Avis Bunnage, Amanda Burton, Anna Calder-Marshall, Derek Fowlds, Philip Middlemiss, Robert Stephens

SEX

About Morse and sex there is a revealing moment in *Last Seen Wearing*: 40. Morse is invited to bed gratis by a high-class call girl, a possible witness he has been interviewing. This is the sort of thing that happens to Morse in Dexter's novels. He always refuses and he never fails to regret it later. This time he very nearly says yes. He has been torturing himself with the thought of this alluring woman 'among the wealthy, lecherous old men who gloated over pornographic films, and pawed and fondled the high-class prostitutes who sat

Soho holds no fears for Morse. The sleazier the better as far as he's concerned.

upon their knees, unfastening their flies.' So what holds him back? 'He was a lecherous old man, too, wasn't he? Very nearly, anyway. Just a sediment of sensitivity still. Just a little.'

The Morse of Dexter's novels undoubtedly *is* lecherous. He likes strip shows. He is enthusiastic if an investigation – such as happens in *Last Seen Wearing*, *The Riddle of the Third Mile*, and *Death is Now My Neighbour* – takes him into Soho and the tacky world of peep-shows, strippers and call girls and on these occasions he generally makes sure that he, and not Lewis for once, does the necessary legwork. On one occasion, however (*Last Seen Wearing*: 8), they are in a strip club together:

> There were gimmicks a-plenty: fans, whips, bananas and rubber spiders; and Morse dug Lewis in the ribs as an extraordinarily shapely girl, dressed for a fancy dress ball, titillatingly and tantalizingly divested herself of all but an incongruously ugly mask.
>
> 'Bit of class there, Lewis.'

Morse is sexually aroused by stripping. The word 'unbuttoning' – as he reminds himself in *The Secret of Annexe 3*: 12 and elsewhere – is a highly erotic word to him, as it was to one of his favourite poets, Philip Larkin. He also, with a slight sense of shame, is attracted to PORNOGRAPHY.

Morse does occasionally take a woman to bed. It certainly happens at the end of *Death is Now My Neighbour* and apparently also with the religious Emma Pickford in *Fat Chance*. Sex also seems to be on the cards with the nursing sister, Sheila McLean, in the last chapter of *The Wench is Dead*, when Morse suddenly decides to double back and spend the night in Derby, where the former dragon of the JR2 is now working. But these occasions are far out-weighed by the moments of disappointment, when Morse sets out again and again to tread the path of dalliance, only to find it leads nowhere near a bedroom.

SHELDONIAN THEATRE

Specifically built as a temple to Oxford learning rather than to any more familiar forms of drama, the Sheldonian is in Broad Street. Based on the theatre of Marcellus in imperial Rome, it is named after Bishop Gilbert Sheldon, who commissioned it shortly after the Restoration of Charles II in 1660. The building, whose interior is made of wood painted to look like marble, is admired by Morse and Lewis in *The Last Enemy*, at a moment when Morse seems to have fallen under the influence of the OXFORD DISEASE at its most virulent.

> MORSE: Look at that.
> LEWIS: Sir Christopher Wren, 1669.
> MORSE: Well done, Lewis. And the place where the Sheldon Lectures are delivered in front of the great men of the university in all their robed finery. To be the centre of attention in such a place, to have your peers hanging on your every word. Worth killing for, would you say, Lewis?

The Sheldonian Theatre was designed only for the performance of Oxford's highly formal and arcane academic rituals.

LEWIS: I don't know, sir. I was once meant to speak in a balloon debate in my first year at secondary school, but it was cut short by a fire drill.

Lewis's inspired *non-sequitur* nicely deflates his boss's rhetoric, but the hubris of the Oxford Disease is on show again at the Sheldonian in the form of Chancellor Lord Hinksey in *Twilight of the Gods*, lamenting the days when all crimes committed on university premises – including, he seems to be saying, murder – were investigated not by the police but by the corps of disciplinary dons, the proctors, and their bowler-hatted enforcers, the 'bulldogs'.

The roof of the Sheldonian, which is open to the public, gives magnificent views across Oxford.

SILENT WORLD OF NICHOLAS QUINN, THE (novel, 1977)

The murderous setting of Dexter's third Morse novel is the office of the FOREIGN EXAMINATIONS SYNDICATE. It lies close to the centre of Oxford and its business is the setting of school examinations at secondary level, on the British pattern but for schools all over the world. When Nicholas Quinn is appointed to join the other four graduate staff members, the secretary, Bartlett, has misgivings, feeling that Quinn's profound deafness may hinder his work. But the appointments board overrules him on the grounds that the new man's impressive lip-reading adequately compensates for his disability. As it turns out, it is Quinn's lip-reading that dooms him.

Dexter is working here with two elements he knows well: he himself is deaf and he worked for many years at a public examinations board in Oxford. Around these two elements he constructs a puzzle which shares some of the elements of a classic 'locked-room' mystery, although it more resembles a Cluedo-type problem. Virtually all the Syndicate staff are suspects, and each of them has to be systematically (and in one case violently) eliminated from the inquiry.

As always with Morse, the tougher the problem, the happier he is at the outset. But from time to time the mood darkens as he glimpses the tragic roots of the crime of murder. Quinn's disability had put him a furlong behind the rest of the field in the career stakes, but with courage and determination he overcame the handicap first as a successful schoolteacher and then in the much-coveted post of examinations administrator.

Yet this courage was also his downfall, as Morse comes to appreciate after much beer-fuelled cerebration. He uncovers a plot within the syndicate to betray examination questions in advance. Quinn, too, had discovered this when he watched a conversation between two of the conspirators who were confident they could not be overheard. But an inescapable flaw in Quinn's lip-reading technique means he makes one misinterpretation, which proves to be a simple but absolutely fatal one.

Morse's task is to solve an interlocking series of difficult puzzles. Things begin to fall into place when, as in *Last Bus to Woodstock*, he discovers a clue concealed in an apparently innocuous letter.

SILENT WORLD OF NICHOLAS QUINN, THE (TV film)

The variations made in this faithful, atmospheric adaptation of Dexter's novel are minor details, such as the fact that Quinn lives in a cottage not a flat and (much to Morse's delight) Ogleby is a distinguished CROSSWORD setter.

First transmission 13 January 1987
Writer Julian Mitchell
Director Brian Parker
Cast includes Barbara Flynn, Michael Gough, Roger Lloyd Pack, Clive Swift, Frederick Treves

SINS OF THE FATHERS, THE (TV film only)

'Death always makes people close ranks . . . Death and money,' Morse tells Lewis as he explains his thinking into the murder of company managing director Trevor Radford. Morse has what should be a congenial task here, since the murdered man was in charge of a family brewing business, a traditionally minded concern threatened with takeover by an ultra-modern conglomerate run by Morse's old Oxford friend George Linacre (John Bird). The Radford family does indeed finally close ranks, but by then it is too late. The large house surrounded by lawns and walled gardens, the butler and other servants, are about to be swept away.

This is not just because Radford's Brewery has lost out in the pragmatic, unsentimental world of competition and acquisition represented by Linacre. The seeds of its destruction were sown in the distant past when the founding nineteenth-century Radford fell out with his partner Ebenezer Knox and ran him out of Oxford. But Knox's heir has come

Morse interviews the grieving widow in The Sins Of The Fathers.

back, determined to secure his share of the business or, if not, his pound of flesh. Like characters in a Chekhov play, the more the Radfords try to shore up their way of life, the more doomed it becomes.

Oddly, Morse's love of beer is never developed by Jeremy Burnham's script into a determining factor in the story. Distaste for MODERN LIFE and the love of beer are two of Morse's ruling passions and, just as the attempted murder of an opera star galvanizes him into action in *Twilight of the Gods*, you would expect him to be similarly charged with energy and anger when a 150-year-old brewery and its product – described (not by him) as 'one of the finest real ales in the country' – are threatened. As it is, we never so much as hear Morse's opinion of Radford's product; the company might as well have been manufacturing computers for all Morse seems to care about its fate.

The only possible explanation is his dislike of the CLASS attitudes of people like the Radfords. Despite what their product means to him, he is not really sorry – except at the level of human sympathy – to see them destroy themselves. And this is what they do: the closing of ranks which Morse observes as a reflex move, cannot save them.

First transmission 10 January 1990
Writer Jeremy Burnham
Director Peter Hammond
Cast includes John Bird, Isabel Dean, Lisa Harrow, Lionel Jeffries, Alex Jennings, Betty Marsden, Kim Thomson

SMALL, DIOGENES

This mysterious essayist, artist and letter-writer (whose dates are 1797–1812) supplies chapter EPIGRAPHS in several Morse books. 'All modern architecture is farce,' is one of his more pithy observations. In the short story 'The Inside Story' his book *Reflections on Inspiration and Creativity*, found by Morse and Lewis on a murdered woman's bedside table, supplies the key which might unlock the mystery, provided Morse can locate the keyhole.

If the dates of Small's birth and death can be relied on, he was an astonishingly precocious and prolific thinker, producing in his short life an *Autobiography*, discourses on *Genius*, and on *The Gamesman*, essays on manners, history and the liberal arts and enough letters on various subjects for a printed collection. These works are exceedingly hard to find nowadays, not even appearing in the catalogue of the Bodleian Library. But various quotations from them can be found in N. C. Dexter and E. G. Rayner, *Liberal Studies: An Outline Course* (1964) which illustrate the full range of his reactionary idiosyncrasies. 'History,' he thought, 'is rather the proper employment of the material we possess than the discovery of fresh.' Another of his opinions – astonishing in one who died when still a schoolboy – is that 'the habitual ministering of the rod at proper intervals is the best mode of education'.

Such draconian methods of discipline were perhaps not sufficiently practised on Small himself, for, shortly after succeeding to the title of Viscount Mumbles, he died by public execution. The nature of his offence is not recorded. He is probably related to Simon Small (dates unknown), whose entry on St Anthony of Egypt from *An Irreverent Survey of the Saints* is quoted in *The Daughters of Cain*: 59. According to Small, this St Anthony mortified himself by lying, hands manacled, in an 'appropriately transparent' sack and ordering naked women to be paraded before him. Simon Small may also be the author of *Small's Enlarged English Dictionary*, which ran to at least twelve editions and provides a definition of 'pension' at the head of *The Daughters of Cain*: 1 ('monies grudgingly bestowed on ageing hirelings after a lifetime of occasional devotion to duty').

SMOKING

For Sherlock Holmes tobacco was an essential part of the thought process and by this one can deduce that Holmes was an inveterate nicotine addict. What of Morse? He certainly does smoke – indeed he frequently feels the very sharp pull of the tobacco habit. But, from the first book, Dexter insists that he is not a slave to the weed. This seems confirmed in the television series, when Morse, although he constantly drinks, is never once seen to smoke.

SPORT

The remark by George Orwell, quoted in *The Secret of Annexe 3*: 5, sets out to show the disreputable nature of what should on the face of it be an innocent pastime: 'Serious sport has nothing to do with fair play. It is bound up with hatred, jealousy, boastfulness and disregard of all the rules.' Morse would agree with this. Crime is, by definition, 'foul play', and he thinks the same of sport.

Morse books and films are hardly bursting with sports, but when they are seen it is never in the most flattering of lights. Golf is played ineptly by Superintendent STRANGE (*Death is Now My Neighbour*), thereby showing his foolishness in trying to curry favour with the top brass. In *The Sins of the Fathers* a croquet mallet is wielded expertly by the Domestic Bursar of Lonsdale, both in her game with Dr Jane Robson and later to kill a man with a crack over the head. Football is played by Oxford United in *Service of All the Dead*: 15, watched in the rain by Morse. He has gone there only because Mrs Lewis has told him this is where he can find Lewis, a devoted football fan and filler-in of pools coupons. But Morse drags the sergeant away at half time – 'You've lost this one, anyway,' he says brutally – as they set off to climb the ST FRIDESWIDE'S tower.

As is noted elsewhere, Morse seems once to have been more interested in CRICKET than he is now. He must also have played a little tennis, judging by a casual remark in *The Way Through the Woods*: 23 'In my youth, I'll have you know, I had quite a reliable back-hand.'

STRANGE, CHIEF SUPERINTENDENT

The comedy to be derived from the inter-play between characters is most evident in the scenes between Morse and Strange, where the humour comes largely from the comic differences between these two men who entered the force at roughly the same time. Strange, under the thumb of his wife, addicted to chocolate biscuits and, despite all protestations to the contrary, as soft as Plasticine in the hands of his clever Chief Inspector, can seem a hapless figure when faced with Morse's commitment and – even more – his wit:

> STRANGE: I mean, these management consultants they brought in – they're practically teenagers some of them. Don't know anything about policing. 'Resource allocation,' they say. And 'downsizing'. Downsizing! I've never heard such language in all my life.
> MORSE: They don't want to downsize you, surely, sir. (*The Daughters of Cain*)

More formidable than he looks – Supt. Strange.

But for all his manifest absurdity, thanks to James Grout's skilfully judged performance, Strange has real presence and authority. You can at such times understand how he is the Superintendent rather than the infinitely more clever Morse.

· T ·

TELEVISION

The story of how Morse came to television began in the late 1980s, when Ted Childs, who was head of drama at Central Television, the ITV company based in Birmingham but with Oxford in its transmission area, wanted to find a detective series with which ITV could counter the success of *Miss Marple*, a successful BBC series starring Joan Hickson. It was the idea of one of Childs's PRODUCERS, Kenny McBain, to adapt Dexter's novels – in the first instance *The Dead of Jericho*, *The Silent World of Nicholas Quinn* and *Service of All the Dead*, using SCRIPTWRITERS Anthony Minghella and Julian Mitchell. It was made, until transferring to Carlton Communications for *The Way Through the Woods* in 1995, by Central's film and drama production company, Zenith.

Morse was from the start a high-quality programme, shot on 16mm film rather than videotape and consequently having a much deeper and richer visual beauty than is common. The revolutionary aspect of *Morse* was its two-hour format, a brave act of faith in the idea and the staying power of the audience. This faith was rewarded: more than 13 million watched the first film and audiences grew from there to 18 million.

Morse himself, of course, doesn't even own a television set and would certainly rather be at an opera, a pub, a lecture or even a football match than watch a police drama on the box.

THAW, JOHN

The actor who plays Morse was born in Manchester in 1942. Although he has worked for both the National Theatre and the Royal Shakespeare Company, it was television that made him famous. Thaw's first regular starring appearance on screen was in the now largely forgotten series *Redcap* (1965–6) but he made his name in fifty-three episodes and two feature films of *The Sweeney* between 1974 and 1978. Just as in *Morse*, Thaw played a police inspector with a sergeant sidekick (Denis Waterman), but the Flying Squad series was fast-paced and frequently violent, and 'Steely' Jack Regan came over as a pugnacious, uncompromising rough diamond, a hard man with little time for the finer things in life. Although there are similarities between the characters – two unorthodox 'naughty boys', tolerated because they get results – it is hard to decide which is the less probable scenario: Regan buying tickets for a Berlioz opera or Morse leading a high-speed car chase followed by a shoot-out.

Stepping into a different branch of the law as Kavanagh QC, John Thaw grows his hair longer and acquires a north-country accent.

The *Morse* series, then, involved Thaw in a change of pace from *presto* to *adagio*, and of key from major to minor. It was clearly an agreeable change for Thaw (he has continued in this more leisurely vein with *Kavanagh QC*) and it is hard not to conclude that in portraying TV's most popular detective he has found the raw materials for the characterization within himself.

THERAPY

Self-help and psychotherapy are ideas about which one would expect Morse to have a jaundiced view, and so it proves. Freddie Galt, proprietor of the Think Thin health farm in *Fat Chance* and Russell Clarke's theory of self-affirmation and 'burning the past' in *The Death of the Self* are both lampooned.

For Morse therapy is only likely to work if it is ALCOHOL-related: a few pints of beer in a quiet PUBLIC HOUSE, followed by some whisky and Wagner at home in the company of either an attractive thirty-something woman or a good book – probably HOUSMAN's *Collected Poems*.

TOWN HALL, OXFORD

This gloriously neo-Jacobean building is in ST ALDATE'S and dates from the 1890s. The centre of Oxford's civic government – the temple of Town rather than of Gown – it is the scene of the performance of *The Magic Flute* in *Masonic Mysteries*. It is also the setting for the ball at which Morse steps out with Dr RUSSELL in the first scene of *The Secret of Annexe 3*, before they are interrupted by Lewis with news of a murder close by.

TURF TAVERN, THE

In this famous Oxford PUBLIC HOUSE and beer garden, situated at St Helen's Passage and Bath Place in a maze of alleyways below New College, scenes in *Service of All the Dead* and *The Silent World of Nicholas Quinn* were filmed. In *The Daughters of Cain*: 15 Morse and Lewis come here to discuss in a 'blessedly music – muzak – free environment' the case under investigation, and in particular the traditions of WOLSEY COLLEGE.

The ball at the Oxford Town Hall where Morse dances with Dr Grayling Russell.

Sir John Gielgud in his element as Lord Hinksey, Chancellor of the University, in Twilight of the Gods.

TWILIGHT OF THE GODS (TV film only)

The final film of the seventh series, which takes its name from Wagner's Götterdämmerung and originally intended as the last *Morse* ever, begins with Morse attending a masterclass held by the (in his opinion) incomparable diva Gwladys Probert (Sheila Gish). He is such a fan that he arranges to have two dozen roses sent round to the dressing room of this 'Welsh singing bird' before her concert the next evening. But first there is the ceremony, in which La Probert will be invested with an honorary doctorate alongside Andrew Baydon the millionaire businessman (Robert Hardy).

The university feels sorry for itself in this episode: professorships are frozen and development projects are placed on hold, while the likes of Baydon are wooed with honorary doctorships in return for large endowments. But Mitchell's script argues that the university risks moral diminishment worse than the financial one by taking cash from such people. Baydon is a monster who expects to be treated like a god: his whole character appears to be modelled on that other Oxford resident, the late Robert Maxwell. Gwladys Probert, who walks alongside him in the cap-and-gown procession along the Broad, is little better: a scheming harridan who preys on her sister's boyfriends. When, processing to the SHEL-DONIAN, the singer is shot by an unknown gunman, Morse has to determine whether his favourite interpreter of Wagner was the gunman's target or Baydon. There is no shortage of evidence to support both possibilities.

Rich in allusion and theme, lushly photographed, this is one of the most exuberant of the *Morse* films. But it poses tough questions about the relationship between life and art, as well as between celebrity and moral worth. These are matters which have always hovered around the world of Morse. But in case it is all too academically rarefied – and symptoms of academic arrogance, the OXFORD DISEASE, are rife in this film – Lewis sees the issue in a down-to-earth idiom all his own: 'My dad used to love football, but he didn't like footballers. You have to keep people who do things apart from what they do. That's what he said.'

Morse is certain Lewis's father was right.

First transmission 20 January 1993
Writer Julian Mitchell
Director Herbert Wise
Cast includes Jean Anderson, Julian Curry, John Gielgud, Sheila Gish, Robert Hardy and the voice of Susan McCulloch

TYPEWRITERS

The fact that all typewriters have unique characteristics leads to ninety-three of the machines in LONSDALE COLLEGE being checked in *Last Bus to Woodstock*: 21, in case any of them was used for the letter in CODE received by Morse's suspect. Two of the Lonsdale typewriters are impounded by Sergeant Lewis for further checking in *The Riddle of the Third Mile*: 14. Morse has an old-fashioned machine of his own with so many typographical idiosyncrasies that when Lewis uses it in *The Way Through the Woods*: 69, he at once spots his boss as the author of the 'Swedish maiden' verses sent to *The Times*.

By the late 1980s typewriters were almost universally replaced by computer word-processors. Morse regards the change as one of the curses of MODERN LIFE, not least because it removes a valuable source of clues in detective work.

DR RUSSELL: Guns are as distinctive as typewriters . . .

MORSE: Not like those blasted word-processors. Robots used by robots – you can't tell the difference. (*The Last Enemy*)

· U ·

UNION SOCIETY, THE OXFORD

This is not a students' union but a debating society in whose St Michael's Street premises many a celebrated, and not so celebrated, wrangle has been staged since its foundation in 1813. Debates are on Thursday or Friday evenings in term time and famous guest speakers are regularly invited. At the beginning of *The Infernal Serpent*, Morse is hurrying through the rain to catch the ecological hero Julian Dear's speech at a Union debate on the environment, but Dr Dear's sensational revelations go unheard as he is murdered on his way there. The only *Morse* scene shot in the Union is in *Greeks Bearing Gifts*, when Morse catches the tail end of a poorly attended talk in the debating chamber on Greek triremes, given by the former academic blue-eyed boy Dr Randall Rees.

UNIVERSITY AND THE COLLEGES, THE

'I can see the colleges, but where is the university?' The philosopher Gilbert Ryle once used this naïve tourist's question as an example of a Category Mistake. The university is indeed a more nebulous, diversified entity than a college, but as we see in *Twilight of the Gods*, it is a reality, with a structure and administration led by the Chancellor (wonderfully played by Sir John Gielgud), the Vice-Chancellor (played by Alan David) and a large web of faculties, examiners, proctors and other eminent officials and bodies. But the colleges are nevertheless self-governing bodies and jealous of their independence. LONSDALE COLLEGE is the most frequently recurring in Morse's world, but there are others, such as COURTENAY (*The Ghost in the Machine*), WOLSEY (*The Daughters of Cain*), BEAUMONT (*The Last Enemy*), BEAUFORT (*The Infernal Serpent*) and ST SAVIOUR'S (*Fat Chance*) all from the films and all with names not immediately familiar from the Oxford University Register.

The Daughters of Cain shows Oxford shaking its begging bowl. An important theme of this film is the colleges' and the university's impoverishment. An incredulous Morse is contacted by a Lonsdale undergraduate as part of a telephone appeal for financial support and subsequently Dr McClure describes the university as 'looking more and more like an ancient down-at-heel uncle. Someone in an old and none-too-clean cardigan whom you ask for Christmas dinner simply for old times' sake'. The President of Wolsey College enlarges on the theme, telling Morse how the college sets about its own Appeal – with personal approaches by Dr Felix McClure to a selected list of the great, the good and the wealthy.

Morse, of course, knows there is something disingenuous about all this begging: 'You know, the university is always moaning about how it hasn't enough money and yet there's always enough for a college dinner for two hundred guests' (*Twilight of the Gods*).

UNIVERSITY COLLEGE

Its chapel was booked for the filming of the funeral of Dr Dear in *The Infernal Serpent*. The fine seventeenth-century windows, with biblical scenes painted by Abraham van Linge, appropriately include a Garden of Eden with the serpent coiled around the tree.

Where's the University? Oxford from the south, showing some of the oldest colleges. The dome is that of the Radcliffe Camera.

· W ·

WAGNER, RICHARD

The most romantic of all German operatic composers was born in Leipzig in 1813 and died in Venice in 1883. His monumental 'music-dramas' attempted to forge a music-religion out of German national feeling and Teutonic myths, culminating in *The Ring* cycle, four huge works, *Das Rheingold*, *Die Walküre*, *Siegfried* and *Götterdämmerung*, which are still played at the temple Wagner created to his art at Bayreuth, Bavaria. Quite why Morse loves Wagner as much as he does – he has been to Bayreuth for his HOLIDAYS and plays the operas constantly – is never spelled out. On a personal level it seems hardly likely that Morse would have enjoyed the company of his favourite composer. Wagner was boastful, financially extravagant (admittedly with other people's money) and thumpingly authoritarian. His POLITICS were racist and his treatment of women serially unchivalrous and exploitative (even his mother was not immune – Wagner once wagered her pension in a card game). None of these features would appeal much to Morse but, as he ruefully learns in *Twilight of the Gods* – the most explicitly 'Wagnerian' of all the TV films – artistic genius does not come with a guarantee of moral worth. Whatever one may think of his personal character, Wagner's music has an almost mystical appeal for many people. It is the antithesis of the operatic tradition of Italy where passion is vital and sudden, like a cascade; in Wagner, emotion flows like lava – slow, hot, viscid and unstoppable. This is not exactly Morse's character, but perhaps he would like it to be.

The composer Wagner, as seen by a Victorian cartoonist.

WARDROBE, MORSE'S

Hardly commented upon in the novels, Morse's frequently rumpled bachelor's clothes are an important part of the way his character is built in the television series. The 'look' was arrived at with several false starts. At one point in the film version of *The Dead of Jericho* he wears a leather coat and leather trilby! At other times he has worn suits that look suspiciously like Armani. But the most recent films have settled down to a Marks and Spencer's look which seems completely appropriate for one who admits this is his favourite store.

WAY THROUGH THE WOODS, THE (novel 1992)

In this novel an irrevocable alteration is made to the world of Morse. Max de BRYN, the 'hump-backed' police surgeon who for years had been one of Morse's closest friends, suffers a fatal heart attack. As he had not yet delivered the results of his forensic investigations into a skeleton found in WYTHAM WOODS, his young (and beautiful) replacement, Dr Laura HOBSON must make Max's crucial, but undivulged, discovery all over again.

Morse is on HOLIDAY in Hardy country when *The Times* publishes some verses, written in the Victorian style and sent anonymously to the police as (or so they are taken by Chief Superintendent STRANGE) a cryptic clue to the mystery of a female backpacker from Sweden who had gone missing in the Oxford area the previous summer. The literary editor, Howard Philippson (counterpart of the real-life Philip Howard), offers his interpretation of the poetry and invites readers to join in with their own thoughts. They rise to the challenge like a flock of starlings, and from the ideas offered it seems that the verses must be by a pub-frequenting Catholic priest torn between the secrets of the confessional and a desire to see justice done, who is an authority on the Pre-Raphaelite painters, drives an A-registration car and admires A. E. HOUSMAN. But Morse's own interpretation of what has become known as 'the Swedish maiden affair', sent to *The Times* under the pseudonym Lionel Regis, is the most detailed and compelling yet.

However, even before he begins to suspect the real identity of Mr Regis, Chief Superintendent Strange has called up Morse to take over from the plodding Chief Inspector Johnson. Finding, not for the first time, that a case has its roots in PORNOGRAPHY, he uncovers a group of men with little in common apart from a shared passion for erotic photography. But this 'innocent' diversion has suddenly got out of control, lurching into violence and death so that now these men are nervous, vulnerable and, in the case of one of them, suddenly dangerous.

As for Morse's own ever-hesitant sex life, we find him making overtures towards the secretive *femme fatale* Claire Osborne before settling for the more reassuring company of Dr Laura Hobson.

The original idea for the clue to a murder published in *The Times* and thrown open to the readers for their suggestions came from real life. During the 1980s the paper received a series of maps and chess notations which anonymously purported to be clues to the burial place of a murdered body. After weeks of correspondence, and fruitless attempts by the police and others to make sense of the clues, the letters were exposed as part of an elaborate hoax. Colin Dexter had discussed these letters with one Sergeant Benwell in an Oxford pub and it is to Benwell that the novel is dedicated.

WAY THROUGH THE WOODS, THE (TV film)

Stripping the novel down to its bare televisual essentials, screenwriter John Madden discards the distracting events in Lyme Regis, the 'Swedish maiden' verses and the deathbed scenes with Max, although Dr Laura HOBSON is again the new pathologist on the case. Claire Osborne, from being virtually a high-class prostitute, is converted into a high-class bookseller, and Karen Eriksson, the Swedish tourist, becomes Karen Anderson, a mysterious English girl with no traceable family.

The most striking elements in the film concern relations between inspector and sergeant, which reach a new low midway through, when all Lewis's frustrations at Morse's persistent belittlement of him bubble to the surface in a furious row. But in the final scene, Morse redeems himself. Lewis, held at gunpoint, is seconds from death when the Chief Inspector intervenes. First he offers himself to the suspect – 'Shoot me. Do it! Do it!' – and then, with a well-timed swing of a shovel to the head, he saves both their lives.

First transmission
5 September 1995
Writer John Madden
Director Russell Lewis
Cast includes Neil Dudgeon, Michelle Fairley, Nicholas Le Prevost, Malcolm Storry

The Way Through the Woods: *Lewis at bay in the climactic scene.*

WENCH IS DEAD, THE (novel, 1989)

In this novel Dexter convincingly reconstructs a Victorian murder mystery and, without resort to science fiction or time travel, sets his twentieth-century detective the task of solving it. The idea behind the eighth Morse novel owes much to Josephine Tey's celebrated *Daughter of Time*, in which a policeman in hospital sets out to solve the case of the two young princes murdered – allegedly by King Richard III – in the Tower. The murder of Joanna Franks on a canal boat in 1859 is not a similarly authentic case, though it is based on one, as Dexter makes clear in the following dedication:

> For Harry Judge, lover of canals, who introduced me to *The Murder of Christine Collins*, a fascinating account of an early Victorian murder, by John Godwin. To both I am indebted. (Copies of John Godwin's publication are obtainable through the Divisional Librarian, Stafford Borough Library.)

It is his stomach that gets Morse involved in this unusual investigation. The epigraph to Chapter 1 runs:

> Thought depends absolutely on the stomach; but, in spite of that, those who have the best stomachs are not the best thinkers – Voltaire, in a letter to d'Alembert.

Dexter's chapter EPIGRAPHS are always skilfully selected, but this one is exceptionally apt. Morse's lifestyle, his use of beer as a prime source of calories, his irascibility and the lack of a reliable emotional and sexual outlet seem to be catching up with him at last, as he is carted off to the JOHN RADCLIFFE HOSPITAL with a perforated ulcer. For a day or two the forces of life and death fight over him, but life finally wins and he moves out of danger, though he continues to need much tender professional care from the sweet and desirable Nurse Welch and her colleagues. When the elderly man in the bed opposite dies – from natural causes – his widow insists on presenting Morse with a copy of her late husband's *magnum opus*, a short monograph for the Oxford and County Local Historical Society entitled *Murder on the Oxford Canal*. It tells the story of a sensational Victorian murder, the death of Joanna Franks, for which two canal boatmen were executed and a third transported to Australia in 1860.

Reading the account with increasing absorption, Morse begins to examine the case as presented by his late co-patient. Victorian POLICE PROCEDURE was not as systematic and thorough as, ideally, it is today, and though Morse's own adherence to correct procedure is (at best) patchy, he finds the chain of evidence in the Franks case woefully incomplete. With Lewis doing the legwork, the librarian daughter of the man in the next bed fetching up details from the Bodleian and a good few nips from the flask of Bell's smuggled in by his faithful sergeant, Morse sets out to find the real solution to the case – 'one of the most beautiful deceptions we've ever come across', as he eventually tells Lewis in triumph.

Joanna Franks begins her fatal journey in a scene from The Wench is Dead.

The essentials of the original Collins case are all present in this novel, though the events have been moved south from Rugeley, Staffordshire, to the Oxford area and brought forward in time by thirty years. This second translocation led Dexter into a solecism. As readers regularly write to inform him, the third defendant's sentence of transportation could not have happened at a date as late as this, such punishment having been abandoned by the British courts in 1853.

WENCH IS DEAD, THE (TV film)

At the time of writing, the adaptation of Dexter's eighth novel – 'radically altered', according to advance publicity – is in production as the thirty-second *Morse* film. The project has reportedly gone ahead without the participation of Sergeant Lewis, since Kevin WHATELY has declined to return to the role after *Death is Now My Neighbour*. Reports that the film will climax with the Chief Inspector's MARRIAGE are not true. (*See also* 'Foreword', and MARRIAGE.)

Scheduled first transmission Autumn 1998
Writer Malcolm Bradbury
Director Robert Knights
Cast includes Lisa Eichhorn, Matthew Finney, Judy Loe

WESTGATE CAR PARK

This gloomy, concrete structure, scene of the murder of architect Michael Gifford in *The Secret of Bay 5B*, is to be found between Norfolk Street and Greyfriars Street and serves the needs of customers in the Westgate Shopping Centre.

WHATELY, KEVIN

The actor who plays Sergeant Lewis came to prominence in a surprisingly popular comedy-drama series about British builders migrating to Germany for work – *Auf Wiedersehen, Pet*. He had previously appeared as a lorry driver dating one of Elsie Tanner's café staff in *Coronation Street* and has subsequently starred as a doctor in *Peak Practice*. He took a supporting role in *Morse* scriptwriter Anthony Minghella's Oscar-winning film, *The English Patient*. More recently he has sought to extend himself beyond the uncomplicated niceness of Lewis and has explored much darker and complex roles. In *Trip Trap* on BBC television, he played a violent wife-beater and, more recently, he has been seen on stage in *How I Learned to Drive*, as a Second World War veteran who is also a paedophile.

The quality Whately brings to the part of Lewis cannot be underestimated. It is an important function of the character to be always asking

An earlier incarnation than Sgt. Lewis – Kevin Whately as Neville in Auf Wiedersehen, Pet.

questions, the better to draw out Morse's own thinking. Whately, however, was determined from the start not to let the character become 'a potato-head', and his mixture of stolidity and intelligent inquisitiveness is one of the great triumphs of his performance. The reason Whately's Lewis is such a popular, indeed essential, part of the *Morse* world is that, while Morse may aspire to be a superman (or at least a superbrain), the sergeant is happy to represent the 'common man'. It is the less rewarding role in some ways, but he plays it with considerable dedication and skill.

WHEATSHEAF, THE

PUBLIC HOUSE in Wheatsheaf Yard off the High Street, where scenes in *The Dead of Jericho* and *Last Bus to Woodstock* were shot.

WHITE HORSE, THE

PUBLIC HOUSE in Broad Street where scenes in *The Dead of Jericho* and *The Secret of Bay 5B* were filmed.

WHO KILLED HARRY FIELD? (TV film only)

Harry Field is a middle-aged painter whose body is found with head injuries in a remote country spot after he has been missing for a week. Piecing together the rackety chaos of his life, Morse and Lewis meet Harry's passionate and sentimental wife, Helen, his elderly painter-father (played in his best expansive style by Freddie Jones), his boozy bohemian circle of friends and a wealthy Eurocrat, Paul Eirl (played by Vania Vilers), who may have been his patron.

They also come across Harry's work, in a bewildering variety of styles that make a pastiche-anthology of famous artists. But according to Morse's friend, art historian Ian Matthews, the work is no good. The truth is that Harry Field was a terrible painter, though a lovely man, an innocent whom people instinctively liked. Even the young single mother on the nearby council estate who became his favourite model, and who knows all about exploitation by 'artists', has nothing but good to say about him.

So what is the connection to Eirl, a man with addresses in three or four countries, including a vast country pile near Oxford? Eirl has a priceless art collection which he is proposing to lease to the British government, but before the deal can be signed Morse and Lewis have uncovered the unsavoury truth about Eirl's collection.

This is the only *Morse* film scripted by Geoffrey Case.

First transmission 13 March 1991
Writer Geoffrey Case
Director Colin Gregg
Cast includes Geraldine James, Freddie Jones, Ronald Pickup, Vania Vilers

WOLSEY COLLEGE

In reality CHRIST CHURCH, Wolsey is the college of Dr Felix McClure in the film *The Daughters of Cain*.

WOLVERCOTE

Morse's late colleague Inspector Ainley lived in Wytham Close, Wolvercote, and Morse visits his widow here in *Last Seen Wearing*: 3: 'The small village consisted of little more than the square stone-built houses that lined its main street, and was familiar to Morse only because each of its two public houses boasted beer drawn straight from the wood.'

Another notable resident of Wolvercote, we hear in *The Wolvercote Tongue*, is Val Lewis's Aunt Cissy. In *The Jewel That Was Ours* and *The Wolvercote Tongue*, the 'Tongue' is part of an Anglo-Saxon belt buckle found during an archaeological dig at the village in

the 1930s. In the film there is a quixotic attempt to return it to the area by throwing it into the Isis from Wolvercote Bridge. A riverbank scene in *Twilight of the Gods*, where the body of the journalist Grimshaw is discovered, was shot here.

Wolvercote has a papermill which supplies paper to the Oxford University Press.

WOLVERCOTE TONGUE, THE (TV film only)

This film, with a fine Holmesian ring to its title, was broadcast on Christmas Day 1987. It is based on one of the detailed storylines produced by Dexter after the success of the first series of film adaptations from his novels. The detailed outline also formed the basis for his novel *The Jewel That Was Ours*, published four years later, but viewers coming to the novel after the film should be warned of some surprising variations. The outcome (at least in respect of the murder of Theodore Kemp) is quite different from the television version. In fact, the solution Morse arrives at in the film – the guilt of Cedric Downes – is also conceived by him towards the end of the novel and he even goes so far as to arrest the man. But (in the novel) events prove he is on the wrong track, so he is then obliged to develop a far more complex and devious hypothesis. We are therefore forced to conclude that what we see on screen is a miscarriage of justice and that T-shirts should be printed and the message 'Cedric Downes is Innocent!' scrawled on walls all over Oxford.

First transmission 25 December 1987
Writer Julian Mitchell, based on an idea by Colin Dexter
Director Alastair Reid
Cast includes Simon Callow, Kenneth Cranham, Roberta Taylor

WOODSTOCK

The site of the first murder investigated by Morse and Lewis working in partnership is a small market town eight miles north of Oxford. In the Middle Ages it had one of the most splendid medieval royal palaces, which was given to the first Duke of Marlborough in 1704 and rebuilt by him as Blenheim Palace. Winston Churchill, the Duke's descendant, was born there in 1874 and buried in nearby Bladon churchyard in 1965.

The name of Dexter's imaginary PUBLIC HOUSE in *Last Bus to Woodstock*, the Black Prince, is derived from the fact that Woodstock was the birthplace of Edward, the Black Prince (b. 1330), eldest son of King Edward III. Since this book was published in 1975, one of Woodstock's other pubs has renamed itself the Black Prince, in a clear case of life imitating art.

WYTHAM WOODS

Pronounced 'Whitem', the woods have been owned by the university since a Colonel Ffennel gifted them in 1942 and are maintained as a haven of wildlife and rare species. They play a central role in *The Way Through the Woods* and *The Secret of Bay 5B*, in which the alcoholic George Henderson works there as a forester.

BIBLIOGRAPHY

In addition to Colin Dexter's books, the following have been particularly useful:

Henderson, Mark, *The Making of Inspector Morse*, London, 1995

Mee, Arthur, *The King's England: Oxfordshire*, London, 1965

Morris, Jan, *Oxford* updated by Mark Morris, Oxford, 1987

Richards, Anthony, and Philip Attwell, *The Oxford of Inspector Morse*, pamphlet available from the Inspector Morse Society, 1997

Sherwood, Jennifer, and Nikolaus Pevsner, *Oxfordshire*, Harmondsworth, 1974

Yurdan, Marilyn, *Oxford: Town and Gown*, London, 1990

PICTURE ACKNOWLEDGEMENTS

AKG Photo Library/Metropolitan Museum of Art, New York): 19

Aquarius Library: 128

The Bridgeman Art Library/Guildhall Art Gallery, Corporation of London: 20

Carlton Television Ltd: 11, 14, 15 top and bottom, 17, 22, 25, 33, 35, 44, 46, 49, 51, 53, 54, 56, 58, 63, 64, 65, 66, 67, 68, 69, 71, 73, 74, 78, 80, 84, 86, 89, 90, 91, 92, 93, 96, 99, 100, 102, 104, 106, 108, 113, 114, 115, 118, 119, 121, 129, 130, 133, 135, 136, 141, 144, 146, 147, 148, 154, 156, 157
(Photographs by Tony Nutley, John Rogers, Peter Bolton, John Brown, David Meadow, Stephen Morley, Ian Pleeth, David Farrell, Simon Mein, Mike Vaughan, John Ridley, Peter Kernot, Tony Russell, Sarah Quill, Richard Blanchard © Carlton Television Ltd)

© Chris Donaghue/Oxford Photo Library: 1, 2–3, 12, 24, 27, 36, 97, 111, 139, 151

Christie's Images: 21

Collections: 23 (© Anne Gordon), 26 (© John D. Beldon), 60 (© Anne Gordon), 137 (V.I.)

G.I. Barnett and Son Ltd (Based upon the 1998 Ordnance Survey Barnett's Oxford Street Plan with the permission of The Controller of Her Majesty's Stationery Office © Crown copyright 88522M): 8–9

Hulton Getty: 79, 152

Image Bank: 123, 149 (Petrified Collection)

Jaguar: 30, 31

Macmillan Publishers Ltd: 52, 88, 94

Mary Evans Picture Library: 38, 41 (Henry Grant), 77, 95, 107 (Arthur Rackham Collection)

The Old Parsonage Hotel: 109

Oxfordshire Photographic Archive, DLA, OCC: 29, 76, 82, 112, 127 top and bottom

Penguin Books Ltd: 94

The Radcliffe Infirmary: 122

The Randolph Hotel: 124